THE LONE WOLF

WOLF #3

PENELOPE SKY

Hartwick Publishing

The Lone Wolf

Copyright © 2019 by Penelope Sky

All rights reserved.

CONTENTS

1

ARWEN

I HAD ONE OF THE SERVANTS PACK MY THINGS INTO SUITCASES AND carry them downstairs.

The only thing I left behind was my pink dress—because I never wanted to look at it again. It would only remind me of the night my husband broke my heart. It would remind me of the night I put my heart on the line and lost my only family.

I gave my bedroom a final look before I walked out forever.

I made it to the front of the house where my black BMW was parked. In the divorce settlement, I didn't ask for anything besides my car and some cash to start my life over. It was only a few thousand euros, just enough to get me an apartment until I picked up a second job bartending or waitressing.

Those bimbos obviously wanted him for his money, but I never had.

If Maverick wanted to continue to be used by women who didn't give a damn about him, that was fine with me.

His loss.

By the time I made it to the car, Maverick had exited the grand front doors and walked down the path toward me. In dark jeans and a gray t-shirt, he looked as beautiful as ever—but I didn't see him that way anymore.

My trunk and back seat were stuffed with my things. Now all I had to do was drive away and forget this period of my life. My first marriage lasted less than a year. Hopefully, my second one would be more impressive.

"Arwen." He caught my attention before I opened the door and got inside the car.

My hand stayed on the handle, but I didn't get inside. The winter breeze was cold, and the ground was muddy from the rain we got the night before. Boots were on my feet, and my jeans kept me warm from the frigid air. With sunglasses on the bridge of my nose, I looked at him. "I'll come by and pick up the papers in a week." I opened the door.

He came around the front then forced it to shut under his palm. "What are you doing?"

"What am I doing?" I asked incredulously. "I'm leaving your ass. That's what I'm doing." I grabbed the handle again.

This time, he blocked it with his body so I couldn't get inside. "That's not what we agreed on."

I laughed because it was such a stupid thing to say. "There's a lot of other things we didn't agree on, too." I pushed him in the chest. "Get the hell out of my way. I owe you a slap, and I'm not afraid to use it."

He stood his ground because a threat like that couldn't scare him. "What are you going to do? Where are you going to live?"

"You aren't my husband anymore, so don't worry about it."

"I *am* still your husband."

My smart mouth wouldn't quit today. "You weren't my husband last night."

He kept up his stony expression.

"Seriously, get the hell out of my way. The last thing I want to do is look at that stupid face of yours. Kamikaze is dead, so I don't need you anymore."

"My father is still out there."

"I'm not afraid of that old pussy." I pushed him again, but he didn't budge. "I can take care of myself."

He slid his hands into his pockets.

"Move."

He stood his ground.

I rolled my eyes then walked around the car to the other side. I crawled in through the passenger door then locked all the doors so he couldn't yank me out of it.

He turned around and banged his fist on the window. "Arwen."

I started the engine and put the car in drive. Then I rolled down the window. "I don't want to be married to you, Maverick. You're the last man I want in my bed. You're the last man I want to look at every day. I'm a big girl who can take care of herself, so don't worry about me."

"Then you should take some more money."

The offer was offensive. I shook my head slightly. "I'm the only woman in the world who doesn't give a damn about your money. It can buy you pretty things, but it can't buy you happiness. I'd rather work my ass off for my shit then take a coin from you." My foot hit the gas, and I drove off, his visage fading in the rearview mirror as I drove farther away. I hit the button and made the window roll back up and kept on going, the entire contents of my life packed in that car with me.

I drove to the edge of the property and reached the main road. The house was still visible in my rearview mirror, and I could see him standing where I'd left him. With his hands in his pockets and his eyes on my car, he waited to see me drive away for the last time.

I turned the steering wheel and hit the gas. "Goodbye, Wolf."

I GOT A FURNISHED APARTMENT. It was small with a single bedroom and a kitchen that was also the dining room. I could only fit a single couch, and my bedroom was only big enough for a queen bed and a single nightstand.

It wasn't luxurious, but at least it was home.

Now that I was really on my own, the weight of everything hit me so damn hard.

Like a pile of bricks had been dropped on my head—and my heart.

I sat the kitchen table with a bottle of white wine as a friend. My lips sealed around the edge of the bottle as I took a large drink. The booze burned my throat and made my stomach tight, but it didn't numb my heartbreak.

I could have ignored his actions if I wanted to keep living there. Most women would probably do that. Keep a cheating husband as long as they got to be rich. But since I loved that cheating husband...that wasn't an option for me.

I sat in the dark and let the tears come to the surface. It was the first time I'd allowed myself to feel the harsh pain. I'd been choking it back up until this point, but now that it was really over, I let myself feel it.

It was like a hammer to the gut.

Tears sprung from my eyes and streaked down my cheeks. My sobs echoed in the small kitchen as I replayed that moment in my head. He walked up the stairs with those two girls at his sides, intending to fuck them in the bed where I slept every night. Our beautiful lovemaking was replaced by something meaningless.

Was I stupid for loving Maverick DeVille?

Was this my fault for letting my heart get so weak?

No...because I thought he loved me too.

I didn't misinterpret what happened. We were together. It felt real. He risked his life for mine, and he was the best husband a wife could ask for. We were intimate, honest, beautiful. I wouldn't trade it for anything else in the world.

Then he threw it all away.

All because I told him I loved him.

How stupid was I?

2

MAVERICK

I sat in my office across the hall from my bedroom. Now that Arwen was gone, I was smoking cigars on a daily basis, and my scotch reserves were slowly being depleted. There was no one nagging me about my health, so I did whatever the hell I wanted.

Abigail knocked on the open door before she stepped inside. In her arms was the pink dress Arwen had worn to the party a few nights ago. It was on the hanger, unwrinkled, like she'd taken care of it. "She left this behind. I can arrange to get it to her. Or if you prefer, I could just throw it away."

I sank in my chair with my fist propped under my chin. "I'll take it to her."

"I can handle it for you, Mr. DeVille."

"No. It's okay."

Abigail gave me a look of pity before she draped the dress over the back of the couch. "Anything else I can get you at this time?"

I brought the cigar to my lips. "Close the door on your way out."

I CALLED HER THREE TIMES, and she never answered.

I knew where she was staying because my men kept tabs on her. She had a small apartment that was walking distance from the theater. It was close to where she'd been living before we got married.

I carried the dress to the second floor then knocked on her door.

Her apartment must be small because I could hear her footsteps so easily. She had a small budget even with the money she took from me, so she could only afford the bare minimum. I stood on the other side of the door as I listened to her approaching footsteps get louder.

She opened the door and looked at me with the same cold expression as before.

I didn't know what I'd expected when she opened the door. Maybe less ferocity now that she'd had a few days to calm down. But she was even angrier than she was when she left my property.

Her eyes glanced down to my hands. "Please don't tell me you came all the way here to give me that."

"What am I supposed to do with it?"

"This." She snatched it out of my hands and carried it to the garbage can next to her counter. She stuffed it inside, getting it stained with the mustard she'd used on her lunch. She pushed it down until it was all the way inside before she came back to me.

That dress cost a fortune. She could have sold it for extra cash.

She looked at my hands again. "Where are the papers? All I need you to do is fill in the little tabs I marked on the side. You do paperwork every day. I know you can figure it out." She crossed her arms over her chest and didn't invite me inside her apartment.

That was when I noticed she still wore her wedding ring. My eyes flicked back to hers. "This is a bad idea, Arwen. You're living in a hole with no one to protect you. My father is still the same psychopath he's always been—"

"I'll take my chances."

"I made a promise to your father—"

"And you have no problem breaking promises. Maverick, get out of my face and don't come back. Sign those papers and drop them, or give them straight to your lawyer. I want to change my name back to Chatel as soon as possible. I don't want to be your wife anymore." She kept up a hard expression and stood her ground even though she was upset. Taking a break for a couple of days hadn't calmed her down at all.

"I didn't break any promises. We've always had an open marriage—"

"Fuck. You." She held her hand in front of my face to shut me up. "It was different, and you knew it was. You could have handed me over to Kamikaze and spared yourself so much grief, but you didn't."

"Because I promised your father I wouldn't."

"You didn't have to pick me over Caspian."

"Yes, I did."

"You didn't have to make love to me like it was all you ever wanted. You didn't have to take me to your bed every night for months. Our relationship was different. It turned into something else, and the second things got real, you turned into a damn coward."

I heard all the insults, but I also heard the pain in between her words. "I assumed there would be times when it was just the two of us. Then we would go back to other people. Then we would go back to each other—"

She slapped me across the face.

I turned with the hit, my cheek immediately reddening because she'd hit me so hard. I slowly turned back to her, surprised she had the nerve.

There wasn't a single regret in her eyes. "I told you I loved you, and your response was to pick up some stupid girls and fuck them. Is that how you treat your wife when she puts her heart out there like that? Your friend? The person you trust? You think that's okay?"

"You didn't tell me. You told the whole fucking room."

"With a romantic song I wrote just for you. I'm *so* sorry for being such an ass. At least I would respect you if you were honest about what happened. But this chickenshit act isn't sexy at all. We both know you ran scared because you felt what I felt. You're incapable of accepting love because you're so screwed up in the head, so you backstab the one person who's on your side, the one person who actually gives a damn about you. If that's your choice, then fine. But I don't want to be married to a prick like that."

My blood was boiling under the skin because of the insults and the slap to the face. But I didn't have a comeback to anything she said. I stood on the threshold while my nerves continued to fire off in distress.

"I don't want your protection. I don't want your money. All I want from you is a divorce." She pushed me in the chest so I would back up from her front door. "Then I never want to see you again."

3

ARWEN

THE SMALL APARTMENT DIDN'T FEEL LIKE HOME.

Not because it wasn't enormous and luxurious like Maverick's estate.

But because he wasn't there.

I lay in bed alone, the covers wrapped around me to keep me warm. My diamond ring still sat on my left hand because I didn't have the strength to take it off yet. He'd come to my door and delivered my dress like there was a chance I'd forgotten it by mistake.

No, I just didn't want it.

Then he tried to justify his behavior.

There was no justification for what he did. I'd laid my heart at his feet, and he stomped it into pieces. He rejected my love and fucked someone else...two someones. It was such a cold response after everything we'd been through together.

I still hadn't gotten over it.

Like it had just happened, I was still crying and cradling the pieces of my broken heart. I lay in the small bed and wished he were there with me. Without his deep breathing as my lullaby, I was stuck in my own thoughts. Every sound outside the window made me jolt. No matter how I tugged the sheets, I didn't get warmer.

I still missed him...despite what he'd done.

Tears burned in my eyes as I stared at my wedding ring. A princess cut center stone with diamonds in the band, it was such a beautiful ring. I became attached to it instantly...and then I became attached to the man who gave it to me.

I'd fallen in love with my husband.

I didn't see it coming, not in the beginning, the middle, or even now. Slowly, the affection deepened into something more. I admired all of his qualities, and as time passed, I became more enamored of the man he was.

Even after he hurt me, I still considered him to be a good man.

Just not the man for me.

I should take off the ring and put it in a drawer. I should sell it at a jewelry shop or return it to Maverick.

But I wasn't ready for that yet.

Until I signed those divorce papers...I was still a DeVille.

I wondered if Maverick was drinking at a bar, trying to decide which woman he wanted to take home. Had he forgotten me so easily? Did he miss me at all? Or did he go back to his previous life as if nothing had ever happened between us?

Was he fucking someone else that very moment?

The thoughts made me cry harder.

4

MAVERICK

I sat at the bar with a drink in my hand. It seemed like that was all I'd been doing for the past week.

Drinking.

Winter hit Florence hard, and the streets were icy with bitter cold. Windows were constantly fogged up, and a heavy jacket was necessary even for the short walk from the car to the bar. Smooth liquor was a requirement to keep the organs warm.

Kent moved into the seat beside me. "She was hot but talked way too much."

"You can't think of a way to shut her up?" There was a mirror against the wall of the bar, so I could see my reflection. My tanned skin was paler than usual, and my eyes were bloodshot from lack of sleep. I'd been smoking too much, drinking too much. Work was pushed to the side because I couldn't focus.

"Of course I could. But she keeps talking about her cats, and it's just a turn-off."

I swirled my drink. "That is weird."

"The hot ones usually are."

Arwen wasn't weird. She was classy, smart, funny...the perfect woman.

Kent pivoted in his chair and studied my face. "You look like shit. Like roadkill on a summer day kind of shit."

I took another drink. "Thanks for the compliment."

"What's going on with you? You've been out every single night this week. Where's the wife?"

I didn't have a wife anymore. I hadn't submitted the divorce papers yet, but she and I were no longer together. I was a free man who could screw anyone I wanted, but I found myself sleeping alone every night. "She's gone."

"What do you mean?"

"As in, she left me."

"She left you?" he asked incredulously. "I thought she had to be married to you."

"Kamikaze is dead, so she doesn't need me anymore." I stared into my glass, my fingers still hugging the sides.

"I always got the impression that she *liked* being married to you."

She did. In fact, she loved it.

If I were honest with myself...I did too.

Kent kept staring at me, waiting for an answer. "You aren't going to tell me the whole story?"

"She left me. What else is there to say?"

"But why?" he pressed. "What the hell did you do? That woman is sex on legs. Why would you screw that up?"

In my eyes, I didn't screw it up. I had every right to sleep with whomever I wanted. She did too. I just chose to exercise that right at the worst time. "We were at a party, and she basically told the entire room that she loved me..."

"So?"

I stared into my glass. "What did she expect me to do?"

"I don't know... Did she expect you to do anything?"

No, but it was awkward. She'd changed the entire dynamic of the relationship when she dropped that bomb. We were just two people together because we had to be. We'd become friends and lovers in the process...but love was never supposed to be in the mix.

Kent leaned against the counter as he examined my face. "Maverick?"

"What?"

"You didn't answer my question."

"No. Because it's a stupid question."

He leaned back then turned his face toward the mirror against the bar. He drank from his glass and let the hostility subside between us.

The silence made me feel worse. The alcohol made me feel worse. Everything made me feel worse.

After a long period of tension, Kent spoke again. "I can tell this is bothering you. You've never been much of a talker, but I can read you pretty well. Whatever happened with Arwen is killing you inside. We both know it. I suggest you make it right."

I pushed my empty glass to the edge of the counter and got the bartender to refill my drink. I pulled it back toward me and took a sip. A haze was constantly over my eyes, like I'd just woken up and couldn't fully gain consciousness. I'd been exhausted since the day she left, even though I hadn't done anything. "After she told me how she felt, I was an ass to her. I ignored her."

Kent stared into his glass.

"Then...I picked up a couple of girls and slept with them."

He slowly turned his head back to me. "That's pretty cold, man..."

"What was I supposed to do? I'm not interested in that kind of relationship. That's obvious."

"Maybe it wasn't obvious to her."

I kept my eyes on my glass.

"So, she left when she caught you?"

"She didn't catch me. I wasn't exactly hiding it..."

"Wow." He shook his head. "You tell someone you're in love with them, and then they bring someone home right in front of you. I'm not a touchy-feely kind of guy, but that would suck."

My fingers gripped the glass tighter.

"Then she just left?"

"Gave me divorce papers the next morning. She packed up her stuff and left."

"And that's it?" he asked. "You guys are officially over?"

"No...I haven't signed the papers yet."

"Hmm..." He took a drink then set the glass on the counter. "Why not?"

I shrugged.

"Did she take half of everything?"

I wished she'd been greedy. It would make it easier to let her go. "No...she didn't take anything."

"What?" he asked incredulously. "She's entitled to half your estate, but she didn't ask for anything?"

"Except her car and a few thousand euros."

Kent continued to stare at me in disbelief, his eyebrows raised in surprise. "Shit...she really does love you."

The only thing she wanted was me. When she couldn't have that, she left. She didn't want to be part of my life anymore. She wanted to move on like our marriage had never happened. I pushed away my glass because I wouldn't be able to drive home if I had any more.

"And you don't love her?"

I stared at my own expression in the mirror, my eyes almost the same color as my scotch.

"You can see it in two different ways," Kent said. "If she doesn't mean anything to you, you got yourself out of a bogus marriage and you have your life back. But if she does mean something to you...you fucked that up pretty badly."

When she threw the divorce papers at me, I hadn't been expecting such a venomous reaction. I knew she would be angry, but I didn't expect her to pack up her shit and leave. She wasn't doing it for a production. She actually wanted to get away from me because being my wife was unbearable to her.

I'd never anticipated the consequences of my actions.

I'd tried to stop her, but she wouldn't change her mind.

My father was still out there, but if he hadn't done anything by now, maybe he never would.

That meant Arwen really didn't need me for anything.

That should make me feel relieved...but relief was the last thing I felt.

"Yeah... I did fuck up."

———

IT WAS ALMOST ten when I arrived at her doorstep. The lights were off, so she was probably in bed already. I raised my fist and tapped my knuckles against the wooden door. I could break through her lock if I wanted to, but pissing her off right away wasn't the best idea.

Especially since she was already pissed off.

Heavy footsteps sounded, and then the door opened.

A half-naked man looked at me, wearing nothing but his black boxers. He was built like a brick house with a hard jaw that no doubt attracted the ladies. With green eyes and a well-structured face, he was a handsome guy. He looked at me with hostility, like he didn't appreciate my visit at this late hour. "Can I help you?"

I was blindsided by his appearance, by his square pecs and tight stomach. With tanned skin like mine, his looks rivaled my own. I'd been replaced so easily, with a man just as good-looking. He may not be rich, but he fulfilled her needs just as well.

He tilted his head slightly and kept looking at me. "I said, can I help you?"

My eyes flicked past his shoulder, and I saw Arwen in the kitchen, wearing his t-shirt with her hair pulled over her shoulder. Her blue eyes were locked on mine, her face indifferent to the events that had just unfolded. She had no idea I would stop by at this time of night, but she didn't seem to care that she'd been caught with a lover.

My eyes turned back to his. "I want to speak to Arwen."

The guy kept one hand on the door and turned to Arwen. "You want to talk to this guy?"

"No." She brought the glass of water to her lips and took a drink.

He turned back to me. "You heard her. Goodbye."

My heart raced as I looked at the scene before me. I'd assumed Arwen was sleeping alone every night, thinking about me. But she was already sleeping around and adding notches to her bedpost. She'd already moved on. "Arwen..."

The guy pressed a hand to my chest. "She said no—"

I grabbed his wrist and twisted it down within an instant. "Touch me again, and see what happens."

She slammed her water glass down then came to the door. "Brandon, give me a second." She grabbed his arm and pulled him away, keeping us separated from each other. Blanketed by his t-shirt, she opened the front door then came face-to-face with me. "Did you bring the papers?"

I came empty-handed—and she knew it.

Her eyes focused on mine, growing more hostile as the seconds trickled by.

I'd come here because I'd had too much to drink. It was an impulsive decision. Now I wished I'd just gone home so I wouldn't have to see that gray t-shirt drown her petite frame. I wouldn't have to smell his cologne on her skin. I wouldn't have to wonder how long she'd been sleeping with him.

"Maverick." She raised her voice. "Unless you have the papers, you have no business being here. Leave."

I should walk away, but I didn't. Rage pounded in my veins, along with an overwhelming sense of jealousy. "Arwen, I'm sorry." I forced the words out even though it was difficult to say them. Knowing she was already sleeping around gave me a sense of urgency I never would have predicted. I never apologized for my actions, even if I was in the wrong. In my eyes, every decision I made was justifiable. But when I saw my life fall apart right before my eyes, I had to do something.

"You're sorry?" She cocked her head as well as her eyebrow. Her arms crossed over her chest, and her mood turned even fouler. "What exactly are you sorry about? For being such a coward? For fucking someone else? For fucking two women? For not facing me like a man and having a big-boy conversation?" She stepped closer to me, as if she wanted to slap me like she did before. "I don't want your apology, Maverick. I just want you to disappear." She grabbed the door and started to shut it in my face.

I grabbed the wood and pushed it back. "I know I didn't handle that situation very well. You dropped a bomb on me—"

"Stop making excuses. You knew I loved you. It was so fucking obvious, Maverick. Don't pretend like you had no idea. All of this happened because you have no idea how to accept someone's love." She poked her finger into my chest. "You turned into a coward. I told you I loved you, and you hurt me in the worst way possible. You used to be the man I trusted more than anyone else. Now I realize you're just weak."

I was taking punches to the stomach, one fist after another. "I didn't handle it very well…"

"No, you didn't. Now we're done."

"I said I was sorry."

"So?" she snapped. "You cheated on me, Maverick. You don't just apologize and make it better."

"I didn't cheat on you—"

She held up her left hand where her wedding ring still sat on her finger. "We were married, Maverick. It was you and me. We had something special. You're telling me that you regularly bed women without a condom? You take the same girl to bed every night? You risk your life to save someone? No. We were married,

Maverick. We were actually husband and wife. Instead of having a fight and sleeping in separate beds for a couple of nights, you took it too far. You did something you can never take back. I forgive you because you did so much for me. But I don't want you back."

My entire body stilled when I heard her decision. She was so repulsed by me that she didn't want me, not even my money or my looks. I was nothing to her, just another man who didn't deserve her love.

She pulled the ring off her finger and threw it at my chest.

It bounced off my frame and landed on the ground between my shoes.

"Goodbye, Maverick." She walked inside then slammed the door in my face.

I looked at the diamond ring on the ground. It was the first time I'd ever seen it without her finger slipped through the band. She slept with it on, showered with it on. She had never taken it off since the day I gave it to her.

But now it was lying on the floor...like a piece of trash.

5

ARWEN

Brandon buttoned his jeans then pulled his t-shirt over his head, covering his muscled frame with a layer of cotton. His hair was messy from rolling around in my bed all night long, and there was still a sleepy look in his eyes. He walked to the counter and picked up his mug of coffee to take a drink. "So...I didn't realize you were married."

He hadn't mentioned Maverick last night. We went back to bed and pretended it didn't happen. But now he'd had a change of heart. "*Was* married." I was wearing my wedding ring when Brandon approached me after the show. He was with a few associates who complimented me backstage. After flirting back and forth, he invited me out for a drink—and I said yes. He didn't seem to care about my commitment then.

"It doesn't seem like you're divorced."

"We got divorced the second he cheated on me."

He set his mug down and kept looking at me.

I poured myself my own cup of coffee. "I'd rather not talk about it, if that's okay."

He was tall and handsome, reminding me of Maverick in a couple of ways. He filled out a suit well and had a nice package. He was a good kisser and a better lover. I didn't compare him to Maverick once because I'd blocked him out of my head for good. Brandon had the prettiest green eyes and light brown hair. He was so pretty that it seemed like he would be married or have someone waiting at home for him. "Fair enough."

"Well, last night was fun..." But now it was over, and I wanted him to leave. I'd gotten a new job as a waitress at a bar just a few blocks from my house. It wasn't the ideal occupation, but it had flexible hours, which was exactly what I needed if I wanted to keep singing. I would never be able to afford anything more than this apartment, but that was okay with me. At least I had a car.

"It was." He ran his fingers through his short hair, looking sexy without even trying. "I'd like to do it again."

It was the polite exchange lovers always had the morning after. "Me too." I stepped away and prepared to walk him to the front door.

"But I actually want to do it again."

I stopped and turned around.

He walked around the corner and came toward me. "Let's have dinner tomorrow night."

"You can't be serious," I said with a chuckle. "My dumbass husband came to the door last night, and you want to keep seeing me?"

"Why not? I'm not scared of him."

He should be.

"And it's ex-husband, right?"

"Yeah..." It would take a while for me to get used to that.

He lingered in front of the door. "So?"

"I'm not looking for anything serious right now."

"I didn't realize eating was so serious." His arms circled my waist, and he pulled me close. "Come on, we'll have a nice meal, share a bottle of wine...and then we'll have hot sex. What else would you rather be doing?"

Images of my life with Maverick came back to me. We had dinner together at the same time every night. Then we went to bed, talked a bit, or watched TV. Then he took a shower, and we ground together underneath the sheets. It was so simple and domestic...but it was beautiful. I shook the thought away and focused on the new man in my life. "As long as it doesn't get serious, I'm in."

"Good." He smiled then kissed me. "I'll see you tomorrow."

IT TOOK me a while to get used to not wearing my ring. There were instances when I would suddenly panic because it seemed like it had fallen off my finger and hit the floor. But then I remembered I hadn't been wearing it in the first place.

I wondered what Maverick did with it.

When he came to my apartment, he apologized for what he did. But that offer felt so meaningless. An apology didn't change the past; it didn't fix my broken heart. It didn't change anything. It was pointless. Our relationship as we knew it died the moment he walked up the stairs with those two women. There was nothing left to talk about.

I wanted a divorce.

I wanted to fall in love with the right man.

I was stupid for thinking it was Maverick.

I performed at the opera that night, but my lungs weren't as powerful as they used to be. A little piece of me died when Maverick hurt me, and I couldn't regain my former strength. There was no drive to be the best I could be. The last time I sang my heart out, it chased my husband into the arms of someone else.

I finished my performance then returned backstage to pull the pins out of my hair and wipe away my ridiculously bright lipstick. I balled up the tissue and tossed it in the bin before I ran my fingers through my curls and tried to smooth out my strands. My car was parked in the front rather than the back because there was no one looking out for me anymore.

I was on my own.

I was just about to rise to my feet when I felt a stare in the mirror. Two chocolate-colored eyes looked into mine, intense and apologetic at the same time. In his grasp was a single red rose.

After Maverick had hurt me, I couldn't look at him the same. When he used to surprise me at the opera, butterflies soared in my stomach. My smile couldn't be contained because it became bigger with every passing second. Such joy would grip me because he was the person I looked forward to seeing the most.

All of that was gone.

I stared at him in the mirror and didn't rise to my feet. "Again, I don't see any papers…"

He walked to my side and placed the single rose on my desk.

When he was close to me, I could smell his cologne. The scent immediately brought me back to the memories of his sheets. They smelled just like him, with a touch of laundry detergent. I rose to my feet and ignored the gift he'd brought. "I have a phone. You could call."

"You never answer my calls."

"Still would save you a lot of time." I moved past him to pull my coat from the back of the chair.

He grabbed my wrist and steadied me, possessing me while a crowd of people moved around us without understanding how intense things had just become. His hand rested on mine on top of the chair, and he slowly came closer to me. "Let's talk in private."

"What is there to talk about, Maverick?" I pulled my hand from under his then picked up my coat.

"A lot of things."

"You had plenty of time to talk, but you chose to fuck instead."

He cringed slightly, like that insult actually wounded him. His gaze fell to the floor, his usual confidence not as prevalent as it normally was. He slid his hands into the pockets of his jacket, and he lifted his gaze to look at me again.

"Why do you keep doing this?" Just when I thought I understood Maverick, I realized I didn't understand him at all. He was the one who ruined our relationship, yet he was the one still fighting for it. But why? "You obviously don't want to be married to me. If you did, you would have said you loved me too, and we would have gone to bed as husband and wife. That option was available to you, but you rejected it. So why do you keep showing up on my doorstep? Why are you here now?"

He stared at me for a long time, ignoring the people walking around in the background. "Let's talk in private."

"No." I wasn't taking him back to my apartment like he was part of my life. He was part of my past now, and that was where he needed to stay. "We had all the time in the world to talk about things when we were together. You chose to push me away. Accept the consequences of your actions and leave me alone."

He kept the same expression, but his eyes narrowed when my coldness caused him pain. His hands stayed in his pockets, and he didn't try to touch me. Cornering me in a crowded room worked out in my favor because there wasn't anything he could do.

"Goodnight, Maverick." I turned to walk away.

He grabbed me again. "Arwen, listen to me."

I pushed off his hand. "Listen to what? What do you want? Don't stand there and tell me you want us to be together because that's never going to happen. You don't get to cheat on me to figure out what you want. That's not how it works. I deserve a man who doesn't have to sleep around to determine what he wants."

"I didn't cheat on you—"

"That's how it felt, Maverick."

"Look, you hit me with some serious shit—"

"I'm tired of going in circles. You keep making excuses for what you did, and that's fine. But if you're trying to get me back, that's not going to work. Your excuses don't impress me. They don't make me second-guess my decision. Nothing will make me reconsider going back to you. I suggest you sign those papers and just let it go. I don't want you, Maverick. You've been dumped."

6

MAVERICK

My week passed with agonizing slowness.

I had the same routine every single day, taking in a few drinks throughout the day. I spent a couple hours at the gym, took care of the cheese production, and then sat in my office with a cigar in my mouth.

The estate was so large that I always felt like a small ant in a large hill. But once Arwen had come there, the place felt a little smaller, a little fuller. She filled the empty halls with her lovely presence.

Now I felt alone in this castle.

The isolation had never bothered me before. I thrived in it. But now the quiet sounds of the ventilation system and the vacuum cleaner down the hall reminded me she wasn't there. Her bedroom had been cleaned out, so there was no evidence she'd been there at all.

Only her memory remained.

Every time I tried to talk to her, her hostility was always the same. She never wanted anything to do with me, never wanted to have a conversation with me. She used to look at me like I was the most important man in her life.

Now she hated me.

I should just let this go. Arwen had made up her mind, and she wouldn't change it. I should move on and forget about it. I was fine before we met. I would be fine now that she was gone. I preferred the bachelor life anyway.

But I still thought about her...all the time.

I still missed her.

I wasn't sure what I wanted anymore. The second things got real between us, my first impulse was to push it away, to sabotage what we had.

Mission accomplished.

Now I was stuck with regret, stuck with the pain of my stupidity.

If I didn't want that kind of relationship, then what did I want?

Without her, what did I have?

———

THE SECOND I walked in the door, she was the most noticeable person in the room. Her hair was slicked back in a tight ponytail, and hoop earrings hung from her lobes, her long, slender neck on display under the bar lights. She picked up a big bottle of vodka and filled the glasses lined at the table.

The men at the counter eyed her like they couldn't believe their luck.

I wanted to grab her by that pretty ponytail and drag her out of there. She only took the job because she needed the money, and the reason she needed the money was because I screwed everything up.

I entered the room and noticed the eyes directed at my wife. Most of the guys stared at her, even if they already had a woman on their arm. Some of the women looked at me, but tonight, I wasn't interested.

I sat at the corner of the bar and waited for her to notice me.

Her tip jaw was almost overflowing—with hundred-euro bills.

This woman didn't even need to strip to get paid like one.

She smiled at a new customer and made him a gin and tonic. A few phrases were exchanged back and forth before she moved on to her next admirer. Slowly, she made her way toward me, running the bar without effort. When she approached my chair and lifted her gaze to meet mine, her smile immediately dropped from her face.

I sat straight on the stool, my suit fitting my shoulders perfectly. I wore all black—the color she preferred to see me in. I held her gaze and hoped she wouldn't pour a drink then throw it in my face.

All eyes were on her, so she didn't cause a scene. "What are you drinking?"

"You know me best."

She grabbed a bottle of the most expensive scotch she had behind the counter and poured it into a glass. She wore a low-cut black blouse that showed off her incredibly beautiful skin. She pushed the glass toward me, fire in her eyes.

I took a drink. "Thank you."

"You aren't welcome." She turned and flipped her hair at the same time, showing her attitude like a pissed-off mare. Then she moved down the bar and kept working, pouring drinks for all the assholes who asked for her number. Her tip jar started to over-flow, but the bills kept getting pushed down.

I sat alone and watched her the entire night, wondering when her shift would end so I could get a few moments of her time. Even though my presence must have startled her, she kept doing her job like nothing had happened at all.

She came back to me, a new drink in hand. "This is from the lady at the end of the bar."

I pushed the glass to the side because I had no intention of drinking it.

She rolled her eyes. "A little late for that, Maverick."

SHE WORKED UNTIL CLOSING.

She served the final rounds, finished the transactions, and then locked the doors when everyone left.

I was glad she didn't bother trying to kick me out.

She returned to the register and wrapped the bills in rubber bands before she shut and locked the drawer. She poured herself an extra shot before she left the dirty glasses in the sink.

I stayed at the counter and kept drinking.

Now that the music was off and the conversations had ended, her heels were audible against the hardwood floor. She slowly walked toward me, the same rage in her eyes as all the other times that she'd seen me. "Alright, I'm tired of this." She stopped at the counter and gripped the edge with both hands. Her nails were painted black, and her makeup was dark and smoky. Black was the perfect color on her, especially when her skin was beautiful like a white flower. "Say whatever you want to say, Maverick. Take all the time you need. Let's finish this conversation so we can move on with our lives."

I finally had the floor, but only because it was the best way to get rid of me. Whatever. I would take it. I pushed my glass toward her then tapped my fingers against the counter.

She lifted the bottle and refilled it.

The lights were low, and the street outside was dark. We were the only people out at this time of night. Everyone else went home, either with a lover or alone. My fingers wrapped around the glass, and I studied the resistance in her eyes. There wasn't a hint of who she used to be. She used to be my closest friend... Now she hated me. "You're right. I can't accept love from anyone. I don't know why... I guess it happened after my mother died. My father has been a hard-ass ever since, and now I've developed some kind of complex."

Instead of unleashing a smartass comment, she just listened.

This was the only chance I would ever get with her, so I wouldn't squander it. "I've never felt good enough for him...so I don't feel good enough for anyone."

"Your father is an asshole, Maverick. Don't let his opinion of you determine your own worth."

"I know, but it just happened." I brought the glass to my lips and took a drink. After I licked the drops away, I kept talking. "We both agreed this would be a marriage of convenience. You needed something, and I needed something. I never expected it to turn into this..." I lowered my gaze. "I've been with a lot of women, and not a single one has meant anything to me. Then I met you... and I started to care about you. Coming from a heartless man like me, that's pretty impressive."

She pulled the glass from my hands and took a drink.

"I knew things were different between us before the party. I could feel it… I knew it was happening. Instead of picking up a woman at the bar, I preferred to stay home with you. You stayed in my bed every night, and I liked it. It felt right. But I wasn't ready for what you put on me…"

She opened her mouth to argue, but then she controlled herself and made her mouth shut again.

"It was a fucked-up thing to do, and I admit that. You told me how you felt, and I was a dick about it. I guess I panicked. I've never wanted to get married, and then I found myself married…really married. I didn't want that. So, I reverted back to what I used to do…"

Her eyes shifted down, like the mention of my betrayal still hurt her.

"I shouldn't have done that, Arwen. Not that it matters…but I didn't even enjoy it. I thought of you the entire time."

She grabbed my glass again. "So romantic…" She brought the glass to her lips and took a drink. When she set it down, she wiped her mouth with the back of her forearm.

"If it matters…I haven't been with anyone since you left." I'd been alone in that bed every night, regretting the stupid decision I'd made. Every time I walked into a room with my wife on my arm, I knew I had the most beautiful woman in the room. But I threw that all away when my emotions got to me.

"No. It doesn't matter."

She'd been sleeping around—and that was a nightmare that kept me up all night long. Knowing another man enjoyed her the way I used to made me sick to my stomach. I knew exactly how she felt when she saw me with those two girls. It fucking hurt. "I have an offer for you."

"I doubt there's anything you can entice me with."

I reached into my pocket and pulled out the black wedding ring I'd only worn once. I'd slipped it onto my finger at the ceremony, but at the end of the night, it fell into my drawer next to my stash of condoms. I held it with the tips of my fingers so she could see it under the dim light.

She stared at it, not breathing for a moment.

I slid it over my knuckle and onto my finger. It fit just as snugly as the first time I'd put it on. "My father still might try to hurt you. He doesn't drop his vendettas easily. You're living paycheck to paycheck and working two jobs to make rent. You still need me."

"I'd rather stand on my own two feet than rely on someone."

I rose to my feet then rested my hand on top of hers.

She stilled noticeably when she felt my touch, and unlike last time, she didn't pull away.

"Let's try this again. But this time...let's do it right."

Her eyes filled with a storm of emotions. She was equally angry and touched. Her fingers shook slightly against mine, but she didn't pull away.

"I promise to be faithful to you, to care for you, and to be your lawfully wedded husband." I repeated my old vows back to her. "We'll take things slow, but this won't be a sham anymore. This is real—from this day forward. I want to try this again...if you'll give me another chance." My fingers gripped hers a little tighter as I waited for the answer I wanted. Now that I was on the precipice of getting her back, I realized how much I wanted it. I wanted to take her home and never let her go again.

Silence passed, and it seemed like she might say yes. There was no venom in her eyes, not like before. But then she pulled her fingers away and dropped her gaze. "No."

My hand went cold.

"It wasn't a sham, Maverick. It was real. And you slept with someone else." She took a deep breath to still the tears that built up behind her eyes. "I told you I loved you...and you didn't say it back. As if that wasn't hard enough... But then you went and did that..." When she couldn't fight the emotion anymore, the tears escaped.

And I felt like shit.

Every time I saw her cry, it made me feel terrible. But never as terrible as this.

"My answer is no," she whispered through her tears. "I've listened to you say your piece. Now please leave me alone."

"Sheep—"

"Don't call me that again." Her eyes darted up, her tears mixing with her anger. "You were supposed to protect me—but you didn't protect me from yourself. You're not my wolf, and I'm not your sheep... Not anymore."

7

ARWEN

I COULDN'T LIE. WHEN HE MADE THE OFFER, I WAS TEMPTED TO take it.

Because I still loved that man.

Despite what he did, I couldn't shut down my heart and turn off my feelings. I couldn't pretend that the sight of his wedding ring didn't mean something to me. I couldn't pretend that growing old with him wasn't something I still wanted.

But I found the strength to say no.

He didn't deserve me.

He didn't love me.

Brandon became the man in my life. He was in my bed most of the week, but we weren't anything serious. He was just the man I used to stop thinking about the man I actually wanted.

Brandon didn't mind since he was getting laid.

I spent my time working my two different jobs. It started to feel routine, balancing two different occupations to make ends meet.

Sometimes, I would perform at the opera then bartend directly afterward.

It was exhausting.

But I would never be able to afford the things I needed unless I kept working.

The longer I didn't have Maverick in my life, the more I appreciated that lifestyle. Without my family inheritance, I had nothing. I was left with the coins in my bank account and the checks my employers wrote. I still had to budget for utilities and groceries, and I could never afford any new clothes.

That wasn't the reason I loved Maverick, so I wouldn't go back to him for that—even if it was the easy way out. Maybe someday, I would be a big star and my salary would be higher. Maybe one day, I could have a nice house of my own.

I held on to that dream and kept believing.

The bar was about to close one night when a familiar face walked inside. Maverick wore a t-shirt and a dark blazer, drawing the attention of all the women in the room. He strode to the bar with one hand in his pocket, and when he reached the spot where he'd been last time, he took a seat.

My heart jumped into my throat at the sight of him. I'd thought I would never see him again, unless he was handing me divorce papers. But here he was, appearing a week after our last conversation.

When I reached the counter in front of him, I noticed he was still wearing his wedding ring. Maybe he took it off the second he got home and put it back on to see me, but I suspected he wouldn't do that.

Proactively, I grabbed a bottle of scotch and filled a glass.

He took it but kept his eyes on me. "How are you?"

"Fine. You?"

He shrugged. "I've been better."

I'd been better too. "Why are you here?"

"Just want a drink."

"All the way in Florence?" He had enough liquor in the house to survive for years without leaving it. Plus, he had servants who would run out and fetch anything he asked for. There was no reason for him to drive all the way to Florence and sit at this bar —unless it was to see me.

"I like Florence."

"No. You like sitting in dark rooms with a cigar in your mouth."

The corner of his mouth rose in a smile. "You really know me."

When I dropped my hostility for a few minutes, it was actually nice to talk to him. I was so lonely in that apartment, even when Brandon slept over. I didn't like to cuddle with him, choosing to stick to my side of the bed. We didn't talk much either because I wasn't interested in his character. He was just a pretty man who knew how to fuck, how to make me forget my husband for a few hours. "Did you submit the papers to your lawyer?" He still hadn't dropped them off, so I assumed he took care of it—even though he was still wearing his ring.

"No." He took a drink then licked his lips.

"Do you need me to do it?"

He shook his head.

"You're going to make this as difficult as possible, aren't you?"

He held his glass by the rim and swirled the contents. "It's my job to do what's best for you...and I don't think divorcing me is the best thing for you."

I rolled my eyes.

"You need a man to take care of you. Living in a shabby apartment by yourself—"

"Don't insult my shabby apartment."

His mouth shut and his eyes narrowed. "A woman like you shouldn't be living alone. My father might be a problem, but even if he isn't, you're a target. Men see you in this bar, and they might follow you home."

"That's what the police are for."

"But the police aren't as powerful as me." He tapped the glass against his chest. "You could be rich and pampered. You could be safe. I can give you the whole world...if you'll be my wife."

"We've already had this conversation, Maverick." Having him as my protective husband in the beginning was a blessing, but I fell in love with him for other reasons. I could go back to him if that was all I wanted from him...but I wanted so much more.

"We're having it again."

"My answer will be the same."

"Then I'll just have to keep trying to change your mind."

I gripped the bottle on the counter and stared at him coldly. Another woman would forgive him in a heartbeat. This was Maverick DeVille...handsome and rich. With that charming smile, he could get away with anything. But I wasn't like other women. I needed more than that. "Goodnight, Maverick."

WHEN I WALKED out of the bar that night, Maverick was hot on my tail.

With my black bomber jacket around my shoulders, I stepped into the nighttime chill. The air was dry and cold, burning my nose the second the frigid air came into contact with the skin. My hands slid into my pockets, and I tightened the jacket around my body.

He appeared at my side. "This is exactly what I'm talking about. You shouldn't be walking home alone in the cold."

"I live just a few blocks away."

"Makes it easier to follow you."

I kept walking, keeping a foot of space between us. "Just leave me alone, Maverick. I gave you the chance to say your piece. I listened to every word. But now you need to let it go. I've made my choice."

He walked beside me, his height towering over mine. His hands were in the pockets of his blazer, and vapor emerged from his nose and mouth. With his height and build, no one could catcall me on the street or bother me. He was bug spray that kept all the gnats away. "Arwen—"

I stopped in my tracks and faced him. "What do you want?"

He slowly turned toward me, sharing the narrow sidewalk with me. There was no one else on the street at this time of night, just us and the freezing cold. "I think it's obvious what I want, Arwen."

"But it's not obvious why. Why do you want to be married to me? You obviously don't love me and you don't want what I want, so why are you wearing your wedding ring and refusing to grant me a divorce? It doesn't make any sense, Maverick. And don't say it's because you want to keep me safe."

His hands stayed in his pockets as he stared at me, the exhalation from his nose looking like cigar smoke. His dark eyes blended in with the night, and he stared at me like a hungry wolf under the bright moon.

"Why do you want this?"

He bowed his head for a moment and stared at the ground. After he gathered his thoughts, he raised his chin. "I like being married to you..."

I crossed my arms over my chest.

"I care about you. I miss you."

"But you don't love me," I pressed. "That's pretty important in a marriage."

"It is," he said with a nod. "Give me some time to get there. I want to try, Arwen. We could get divorced and start over from the ground up, but I don't want to do that. I want us to have what we had before, but to try to make it work in our own way. Truth be told, I don't want to go home with someone else. I don't want to sleep alone. I don't...want to live like this. I know I fucked up, but give me a chance to make it right. I was a good husband to you, but I'll be better this time around."

It was a testament to my love for him that I actually considered his offer. My heart beat for this man in a special way. My family was gone, but I felt like he'd become my new family. DeVille fit me far better than Chatel ever did. I had a husband I respected and admired, someone I cared so much for. I'd fallen in love in a way I never had with anyone else. Brandon made me feel lonely, and every other guy was a poor substitute for what I really wanted.

"Sheep..." He stepped closer to me. His boots crunched against the cold concrete, and his hand gently slipped into my hair. His fingertips brushed against my cheek before he cupped my face. He brought his head close to mine, his lips just inches away.

I melted—like always. There was nothing I wanted more than to abandon my apartment and go home with him. I missed those crisp sheets. I missed his fireplace near his bed. I missed sleeping so soundly because I knew nothing could ever hurt me.

But then I remembered I wasn't the last person to sleep there. Two obnoxious gold diggers had taken my place. With their arms and legs draped around his body, they'd claimed him as theirs. I was so easily replaced.

I grabbed his wrist and pushed his hand down. "I can't forget what you did. I can't stop thinking about it. It makes me want to cry every single time."

He released a deep breath as his hand slowly lowered to his side.

"I want to fall in love with a man who wants to fall in love with me. You may be a good man who took care of me, but that's not good enough. I want commitment, loyalty, and integrity. I want a man who would never, ever hurt me. That isn't you…"

"It is me," he whispered. "Give me a chance."

I stepped away. "No." I turned to walk off.

"Sheep."

I turned back around. "Please don't call me that anymore." He had no idea how much pain this caused me. I wanted to jump into his car and drive to our happily ever after. That apartment would never feel like home, not the way his estate did. Walking away from him was the hardest thing I'd ever had to do. I would never love anyone else the way I loved him…but I had to try. "Bye…"

He stayed on the sidewalk and watched me walk away. He didn't try to change my mind again. He didn't threaten to stay married to me forever. He finally let me go.

Finally let me walk away.

BRANDON WATCHED me pull on my jacket then fix my hair. He stayed in bed, the sheets bunched around his waist. With tanned skin and a pretty face, he was a great man to share a mattress with. "Your mind always seems to be somewhere else."

"Not always."

"No. Always." He got out of bed and started to get dressed. "Divorce is hard...especially when you don't want to get divorced."

"I thought I said I don't want to talk about that."

"You did—but you're always thinking about it." He pulled his shirt over his head then came closer to me. "It's alright. Now I understand that I can't compete with this guy. No one can."

"There's nothing to compete with. We're over."

"You're not over him."

I held his gaze. "I never said I was..." I was sleeping with Brandon so I could forget about Maverick, but the haze wasn't as strong as it used to be. The high Brandon gave me became weaker and weaker every time we were together.

He bowed his head slightly. "Well, I like you. But now I'm starting to worry that you'll never like me."

"I said I wasn't looking for anything serious."

"Yeah, but things change."

It wouldn't change for a long time. I had been with Maverick for over six months. Feelings like that didn't just go away...not easily.

"Can I walk you to work?"

"No...I'm okay." I headed to the front door and grabbed my keys on the way out.

Brandon walked with me until we reached the sidewalk. "You want a ride?"

"No. I'd rather walk."

He continued to watch me like he hoped I would change my mind. He was a beautiful man and it was surprising that he had his attention set on me, but I didn't feel anything. There wasn't that burning chemistry like there was with Maverick. He gave a slight nod before he walked away. "I'll see you later, then."

———

THE BAR WAS quiet that night.

Only a few people were sprinkled at the counter and the tables, mostly couples who'd met up for a drink before bedtime. I kept looking at the clock and waiting for the night to end...even though I had nowhere to be.

When I had nothing to do, I sipped a hot cup of tea with a lemon wedge, resting my voice as much as possible. Singing at the theater and then talking to the customers at the bar strained my vocal cords.

It was just an hour before closing when a group of four men walked inside. I knew something was wrong because they weren't the usual demographic of the patrons who came to this bar. They were all dressed in black—and they were older.

The man in front was Caspian.

"Shit..." My hand immediately reached for the bat hidden underneath the counter.

Caspian was dressed in a three-piece black suit, looking like he belonged somewhere much fancier than a small bar in downtown Florence. He smoothed out his vest as he came toward me, carrying himself just the way his son did. Age didn't inhibit him or slow him down at all. He was still lethal.

The men raised their guns and pointed them at the patrons.

Caspian locked his eyes on me and slowly approached the bar, those brown eyes full of victory.

Even if I bashed in his skull, one of his men would gun me down. I'd lie on the floor in a puddle of my own blood.

His men ran everyone out of the bar, keeping their guns aimed at their heads until they finally left the room. The glass doors were shut and locked.

Now I was on my own.

Five armed men against one bat.

I couldn't even reach for my phone and call Maverick. He wasn't my husband anymore, so I shouldn't want to contact him in the first place...but I had no one else.

Caspian lowered himself onto the barstool and pulled out a silver pistol. He laid the gun on the counter between us, like he dared me to reach for it.

I held the bat at my side.

He must have been able to see my grasp in the mirror behind me, because he smiled like he was amused. "I may be old, but I'm a quick draw. I'll put a bullet in that pretty little head long before you smash that bat into my skull. And it'll take a few hits before you cause any real damage."

"You underestimate me."

"No...I learned my lesson." He smiled in a sickly manner. "Now make me a drink."

My instinct was to defy him because I didn't appreciate being bossed around. But I didn't have any options, not when his four men were staring at me with their guns now back on their hips. I was cornered like a rat, and there was nowhere for me to run. Hopefully, the customers who had just been kicked out would call the police...even though it probably wouldn't make a difference.

When I didn't talk back, he smiled. "We're off to a good start. Scotch—neat."

I grabbed the bottle and filled the glass.

"Pour one for yourself as well. You're going to need it."

I filled another glass and set the bottle aside. The bat leaned against the counter, and I didn't bother holding on to it. I pushed his glass toward him, coming in close contact with the gun. If I were quick enough, I could grab it and shoot him before his men shot me.

But I didn't take the risk.

He brought it to his lips and took a long drink, his eyes staying on me. "Enjoy your new profession?"

"Enjoy putting guns to people's heads?"

"As a matter of fact, I do." He took another drink and licked his lips just the way his son did.

"You came here to kill an unarmed woman?" I shook my head in disappointment. "That seems cowardly if you ask me."

"Taking away a family's justice is cowardly as well."

"No. That was heroic." I only had minutes to live, so now was the time to speak my mind. "I told you I was sorry about your wife, but I stand by my actions. Innocent people didn't deserve to die."

"My wife was innocent." His big eyes stared into mine. His eyes were different from Maverick's, much larger in appearance. They were the same color, hot espresso or scotch.

"And she didn't deserve to die."

He picked up the glass and swirled the contents without watching his movements.

"What now? You're just going to kill me?"

"You don't seem scared."

I was scared. I just hid it pretty well. "I feel bad for Maverick. His own father hunted down his wife and killed her in cold blood."

"Ex-wife, right?" He cocked his head slightly to the side.

I guess Maverick and Caspian were on speaking terms.

"You're living in a run-down apartment and working two jobs to make ends meet. Interesting."

I didn't want to draw this out with useless chitchat. It was my fault for not taking Maverick's warning seriously. If I wanted to live, I should have stayed with him. But after seeing him with someone else, my will to survive disappeared quickly. Now I had to face the consequences of those actions. Maverick would have to carry the guilt of my death forever. "Lots of other people do it. I'm not special."

"But no one would walk away from a rich husband the way you have."

"He was more than just a rich husband..." When I thought of Maverick's qualities, his money never crossed my mind. His success was such a small part of who he was. His good heart was the best thing about him.

"Why did you leave him?"

This man had a gun sitting on the counter, but he wanted to talk like we were friends. "What makes you think I left him?"

"Because my son would never leave you. He played Russian roulette against a madman to save your life. He's been far more loyal to you than he ever was to me. So why did you leave a man who gave you everything?"

I gripped the edge of the counter. This conversation wasn't going the way I expected at all. It was an interrogation about my personal life, not an execution for my crimes. "It's none of your business."

"He's my son—it is my business."

"Then why don't you ask him?" I snapped. "Oh, that's right. You don't have a relationship with him."

His wide eyes stared at me without any reaction.

I took a drink.

Caspian didn't press the question to me again. "My dislike for you is very clear. I didn't like you before you crossed me, and now, I like you even less. But you need to understand what my son has done for you. He's a very good man. Whatever his faults may be, they don't compare to his good qualities."

My eyes softened. It was the first time I'd heard Caspian say anything positive about his own son. It was the first time he'd talked about goodness and love...not hate and murder.

"Give my son another chance. His actions couldn't have been that egregious because he's incapable of being cruel. Not to mention, that man has done everything to keep you safe. He provides for you, protects you. He was willing to put a bullet in his brain to keep you alive. If you continue to focus on his one wrongdoing, then you're a much dumber girl than I realized."

I listened to every word he said, but my mind was also thinking so many things at once. "Let me get this straight... You're here to tell me to forgive your son?"

He drank his scotch.

"You aren't here to kill me. You're here to play cupid."

He lowered his glass, his eyes narrowed at the provocation.

"So, you do care about your son."

He finished his drink and pushed the glass toward me. "My vendetta against you is on pause at the moment. Killing you in your bed while you sleep felt cheap. Too easy. You should be at home with your husband, not sleeping around with whatever pretty boy you find on the street. My son needs his wife." He grabbed his gun from the counter and slipped it into the back of his slacks as he stood up. "But make no mistake, Arwen. When the right time comes, I will kill you. I will slaughter you like a pig and use your meat like a Christmas ham." He rested his hand on the counter between us, his fingers balled into a fist. "Tonight, I'm doing the right thing for my son. But tomorrow, I'm doing the right thing for me."

THAT WAS the strangest conversation I'd ever had—but I took it seriously.

Caspian didn't kill me that evening, but tomorrow was a new day. The conditions would change, and we would be enemies once more. Knowing his son was upset that he'd lost his wife, Caspian had intervened because he wasn't that heartless after all.

But then he turned back to being cold once he was done.

Very strange man.

The next day, I packed up all my things and stuffed them into my car and made the drive back to Tuscany. Caspian knew where I worked, where I slept, and proved he could kill me whenever he felt like it. Living on my own wasn't safe. I needed a strong fence, a security team, and a man who could protect me.

I didn't have another choice.

I drove across the countryside and left my former life behind. My apartment would be inhabited by some other poor person. My job at the bar was abandoned because I couldn't work there anymore, not after watching Caspian's men point guns at everyone's heads. I hadn't changed my mind about my relationship with Maverick, but I looked forward to returning to his estate.

It was home.

I checked in at the front gate, and the guys let me pass through. I knew Maverick would be notified of my return. The guys would tell him that my car was stuffed with my belongings, as if I intended to return permanently. Before I even made it to the front of the house, Maverick would know exactly what my intentions were.

I was a weak person who was unable to take care of herself. I didn't have the strength or the training to fight off a man like Caspian and his crew. I didn't have the cash to buy a powerful fortress that could keep all the assholes off my property. I was just a woman without means. I was crawling back on my knees to a man who cheated on me...because I didn't have a choice.

But deep down inside...I was happy to be there.

As the house became more visible, I noticed a man step out of the large double doors and walk down the path to the enormous driveway. With square shoulders, tall height, and purpose in his gait, he headed down the path and approached the road. He was in a black blazer and dark jeans, and his face became more visible as I slowly approached. With dark brown hair and matching eyes, he was a beautiful man who could easily appear in a cologne commercial.

I pulled up to the house and turned off the engine.

Maverick stayed on the sidewalk.

I gave myself a few more seconds to prepare for the conversation. I was there for refuge because I had nowhere else to go. My family was buried in the ground, and my husband was all I had left. As always, I turned to him...because he was my only family.

I found the strength to get out of the car and face him.

I walked around the front of the car, my eyes downcast because I was ashamed to be crawling back to him. He'd tried to get me back, but I'd rejected him every single time. Now I was only here because I didn't have any other choice. He would either accept me with open arms or turn me away because I was only there because I needed something.

I hoped it was the first one.

When I stopped in front of him, I lifted my gaze to finally look at him. It was a sunny day in the middle of winter, and the clear sky only made the air chillier. It was so bright that sunglasses were needed, but neither one of us carried them. I looked into his dark eyes and didn't see a single hint of resentment. "I'm here because—"

"I don't care why you're here. I'm just happy that you are." His arms wrapped around my waist, and he cradled me into his chest. His chin rested on my head, and he squeezed me like he never wanted to let go.

I closed my eyes because it felt good to be wrapped in his embrace. It was far better than any night I spent with Brandon. The love I had for this man immediately grew the second our bodies were wrapped together.

He moved his lips to my forehead and gave me a gentle kiss.

I pulled away and lifted my chin to meet his gaze. His features were softer than they'd ever been because he was so relieved to see me. It was the most vulnerable he'd ever been, as if he couldn't believe this was really happening. "I want you to know that your father came to the bar when I was working last night..."

His hands loosened from my waist and slowly moved to his sides.

That was when I noticed his wedding ring. He still wore it, even though he wouldn't have had time to run to his bedroom and put it on before meeting my car in front of the house. That meant he'd already been wearing it. "He told me I should come back to you because of everything you've done for me...because you care about me."

Maverick clearly didn't know what to say to that. His father never expressed any concern for him, but now he'd tracked down his wife to fix his relationship. His shoulder visibly tightened as the skepticism entered his gaze.

"He suggested I come back to you...because he still intends to kill me. But he wanted to do the right thing for you first." I still didn't quite understand it, how a man could help his son but still focus on his own self-interest. The gesture was considerate coming from Caspian, but also just as twisted. "That's why I'm here... because I have nowhere else to go. He knows where I live, where I work... I don't have a choice." I didn't want Maverick to think I was there by my own choice, that I wanted to give this relationship a try because I'd had a change of heart.

Maverick's expression didn't alter as he watched me.

"I just wanted you to know that... Do you want me to go?" I knew he wouldn't turn me away, but I wanted to ask anyway. Just as we had been in the beginning of this marriage, we were back to being in an arrangement. I needed something from him, but in this case, he didn't need something from me.

"You want me to protect you from my father?"

I nodded.

"And you don't want anything else?"

"No...my feelings haven't changed." I basically wanted a place to live where I would be safe. I wanted to have the best protection possible. Leaving the country wasn't an option because I didn't have the money to pull it off.

"You can stay with me."

I knew he would take me in, but I felt grateful anyway. He was the only person I could count on.

"But I want us to try again. I want us to try to make this marriage work."

There was a condition for my refuge, a payment for my safety.

"Give that to me...and we have a deal."

8

MAVERICK

WHEN SHE ARRIVED AT THE HOUSE, I ASSUMED SHE'D CHANGED HER mind because she missed me. She forgave my actions because she loved me enough to let it go. Our relationship didn't start off conventional, so the severity of my crime was debatable—especially when I did so much for her. When her car pulled up to the front of the house, I thought that was a new start.

But it turned out my father had threatened her.

She still needed me.

Instead of being annoyed, I seized it as an opportunity. She needed something from me, and I wanted something from her. It wasn't right that my father threatened her, but it did play into my hand well.

Now she was back.

The servants returned her things to her bedroom. Everything was back to the way it'd been originally, with her nice dresses hanging in the closets, her jewelry on the nightstand. Her makeup and hair supplies sat on the counter in her private bathroom. She's been gone for almost a month, but she somehow made the room smell like her the second she walked inside.

I lingered in the doorway and watched her sit on the couch, her eyes distant as her mind lived in some other space. Her fingertips rested against her lips, painted black like her mood. Her hair was pulled back in a bun, a few strands coming loose. Now that she was surrounded by my fortress, she was safe once again, but she looked as lost as before.

Even though I was staring at her for minutes, she never noticed I was there. With her legs crossed and her body tense, she wasn't at ease in her old home just yet. I watched her for a few more minutes before I cleared my throat.

Her head snapped in my direction. After a quick dilation, her eyes relaxed as she took in my appearance. Embarrassed that she had been oblivious to my stare, she turned away, and I noticed her cheeks redden slightly.

"Doesn't feel the same?"

"No, it does..." Her arms stretched across the fabric of the armchairs, and her fingers tapped against the edges. "Feels exactly the same."

"You don't have to stay in here." It was presumptuous to invite her into my bedroom, but I wanted to make the offer anyway. We'd never actually lived in the same quarters before, but I knew I wouldn't mind sharing my space with her. My closet was big enough, and it wasn't like I needed the privacy anymore. Once that ring was on my left hand, I became a married man...a real married man.

"I need my own space." She still wouldn't look at me. Her feelings toward me hadn't changed. Every conversation we had ended the same way, and it seemed like her mind-set wouldn't budge. She told me she would try, but she obviously wasn't ready to put much effort into it just yet.

"You know where to find me if you need anything."

She still didn't turn around to look at me. As if she was picturing my infidelity that very moment, the thought was scarring enough to make her cringe.

Now that she was under my roof, there wouldn't be another man in her bed. When she returned to Florence for work, she wouldn't be sleeping elsewhere. She'd already had her lover, so we were even. "I expect your fidelity, Arwen. You better have broken things off with Brandon."

She slowly turned her head toward me but didn't meet my gaze head on. "That's ironic..."

"I had my slipup, and you had yours. We're even now."

"Even?" she asked incredulously. "Me telling you I loved you then you sleeping with someone else isn't the same at all. No, we aren't even."

"But if we're trying, then we're wiping the slate clean."

"Whoa." She rose to her feet and finally looked at me head on. "I said I would try, but that doesn't mean you get a free pass. I'm still hurt by what you did. It still keeps me up late at night. I appreciate your taking me in, but that doesn't earn your vindication. It doesn't right the wrong you made."

"You're going to need to forgive me, or this is never going to work."

"Well, you can't force me to forgive you. You can't expect me to forget about it overnight."

"But I want this just to be the two of us. That's all I'm asking." It was wrong for me to expect her to let it go so easily. She hadn't taken me back in the first place because it still bothered her. If we were living under the same roof and being monogamous, then she was bound to forgive me in time. I just had to be patient... even though it'd already been the longest year of my life.

Her eyes became less hostile, and she turned away. "Alright…"

THE MEN DIDN'T SHOOT me on sight, so they obviously expected me to show up at some point.

I entered the grounds then stepped through the main door. My childhood home was exactly the same, distinctly nostalgic. Dark hardwood was under my feet, and there was charcoal trimming along the floors and ceiling. It hadn't changed since my mother had spruced up the place. My father would never make a single change for the rest of his life.

My father was sitting in the living room when I walked inside, a cigar smoldering in the ashtray. He was drinking with one of his men. A bottle of scotch sat in the center of the table, and their glasses were both full of another round.

He looked up at me—dark eyes identical to mine. "You looked a lot better in that suit you were wearing the last time I saw you."

I took a seat on the leather couch and glared at the man across from me. He was the head of security, but he was chummy with my father. He handled my glare as much as possible before he finished his glass and dismissed himself.

My father pushed the bottle toward me. "You can have that. I'm sure you don't need a glass."

I wasn't in the mood for his games. "You threatened my wife."

He tilted his head slightly and shrugged. "Not quite. I told her she should go home to her husband. *Then* I threatened her."

"Doesn't matter what the order was."

"I think you should be thanking me. She's home because of me, right?"

I had no idea how I would have gotten her back otherwise.

"She needed to be reminded of her station. She needed to remember what she was losing by walking away."

"She's too good for me, and we both know it."

"I don't know about that," he said with a chuckle. "But I can tell that woman loves you...and I can tell she means a great deal to you. Whatever your differences are, you could work them out. I doubt she left just because Kamikaze is dead...which means you screwed it up at some point."

"How would you know if she loves me?" I doubted Arwen blurted that out when he had a gun pointed at her.

"Because I was there."

I ignored the bottle of scotch he'd offered me. When I thought about the moments when it was obvious how she felt about me, there was no one else in the room. It was us together in the shower, deep under the sheets, or just looking at each other across the table.

"I was there when she played that song for you...in case you don't remember."

After everything that had happened with Arwen, the details of that night slipped my mind. I barely remembered the conversation I had with him at the bar. It wasn't much of a conversation because he didn't say a word.

"I had more important things on my mind."

"Clearly..." He shook the ice cubes in the glass and took a drink.

"So you openly admit you want to kill the woman who loves your son?"

He shrugged. "Wouldn't have to be this way if she hadn't gotten in my way."

"You should thank her. She stopped you from doing something you would have regretted."

"I don't regret anything."

"Really?" I asked bitterly. "You should regret getting involved with Ramon in the first place. That's the reason Mother got killed. All of this happened because of *you*. You may have lost your revenge because of Arwen, but all of this happened because of you. Stop putting the blame on other people, and put it where it belongs." I rose to my feet, sickened by the empty look in his eyes. "Stay away from my wife. If I see you anywhere near her, I'll kill you. And I mean that."

He lifted his gaze to look at me, his elbows resting on his knees.

"You didn't protect your wife the way you should have. I won't make the same mistake." I turned away and left the living room, knowing full well I could pull out my gun and shoot him right between the eyes. When faced with a loaded pistol across from Kamikaze, I didn't hesitate to compete in a deadly match of Russian roulette. I certainly wasn't afraid of anything—like pulling the trigger. But even now, I still couldn't put a bullet in his brain and watch the light leave his eyes. I hated myself for that.

"Maverick?"

My feet halted on their own even though I wished I could keep walking. I wished this man didn't have any effect on me, that he didn't have this invisible power over me. In my eyes, he was still my father, the man who raised me. I slowly turned back to him. "Do what you have to do. Just know I'll do the same."

ARWEN SPENT her time in her bedroom for the next few days. She watched TV in her living room, had meals by herself, and rarely ventured out unless she went to work in Florence.

As much as I wanted more from her, I kept being patient.

I spent my time at the gym and working in my office. My thoughts always strayed to the woman living in my house, the woman who wanted nothing to do with me. Ever since she'd come into my life, she complicated things. My relationship with my father was never the same. Even my relationship with myself wasn't the same either. There was no one else who could make me face Kamikaze in a standoff like that, but she made me do the most unexpected things.

Now, we were a million miles apart.

She still despised me for what I did. My infidelity was a sign of betrayal, a stab to the back. We were so close, and just when we got closer, I pushed her so far away that she never wanted to come back. The unconditional love that used to be in her eyes was long gone, like the sun that set over the horizon. Sometimes there were hints it was still there, but in the end, it was just the memory of the sun's rays that reflected in my mind.

My behavior had been thoughtless and stupid. It was that much stupider because I didn't even want to sleep with anyone else. I'd forced myself to do it just to make a point...even though I didn't even remember what that point was. When faced with something as intimate as Arwen's feelings, I didn't have the capacity to accept it. Anytime I had ever loved anyone, I lost them. The more you cared, the more you had to lose. I'd liked our relationship the way it was, and I didn't want it to change.

But it changed anyway.

Now a wedding ring sat on my left hand, and I was committed to one woman for the rest of my life. Well, as long as she would have me. This was supposed to be a means to an end, but somehow it became very real.

Arwen was really my wife—not just on paper.

Now, I wished I could go back in time and punch myself in the face instead of picking up those women.

I understood why she was upset about it. I understood why she didn't look at me the same. But I wanted her forgiveness anyway.

After her silence had lasted several days, I returned to her room in the hope of a conversation. Even if she just wanted to tell me off, I preferred that over her lack of communication. The bedroom door was open, so I stepped inside.

She sat on the couch and wrote in a small notebook. Her pen danced across the pages as she added her words with beautiful penmanship. The format of the lines resembled a poem, so I wondered if she was writing a story.

I let myself inside and allowed my footsteps to announce my presence.

She tore her gaze away from her notebook and looked at me. As if no time had passed at all, she was still ice-cold.

I could talk about the distance between us, but since that had failed so many times, I decided to focus on something else. "What are you working on?"

Her body had been rigid just moments before, and it took a few seconds for her to relax. There would be no interrogation about our relationship, and that made her thaw just a bit. "A song."

She didn't invite me, but I took a seat in the armchair across from her. "Can I hear it?"

"It's not done. These are just the lyrics. I don't have any music for it."

"How's it coming along?"

She closed the notebook and capped the pen. "Pretty well until you came along."

I missed the camaraderie we used to share. We were friends and allies. I would even say she was my closest friend. But that comfortable relationship had been replaced by standoffish expressions and cold comments. "I talked to my father the other day."

She set the notebook on the counter beside her. "How'd that go?"

I shrugged. "He's still a psychopath…"

"Some people never change, huh?" She tossed the pen on top, and it rolled toward the edge of the table.

"Seems that way."

"Do you want to talk about it?"

I just wanted to talk to her, even if we discussed a subject I hated. "He doesn't make any sense. He told you to come back to me because that's what I needed. But he also still intends to kill you. His warped mind can separate the two like they're distinctly different when they aren't."

"I don't understand it either." She crossed her legs and rested her fingertips against her lips. It was a cool evening, so she was in black leggings and a loose-fitting sweater while the gas fire roared in the hearth underneath the TV. Her hair was styled, but her makeup was gone. She looked ready for bed, and that was when she looked the most hypnotizing. The fatigue in her eyes was sexy. Her body was relaxed and should have been draped over something—like me. She became more vulnerable, too tired to fight any obstacle that might get in her way. If she was dressed like that, then that meant she was cold sleeping without me.

Maybe I should take all the covers off her bed so she'd be forced to sleep with me…or freeze.

"When he came to the bar, I was surprised by everything he said. It was the only time I've ever heard him say something nice about you."

"Nice?" My father was capable of saying something nice?

"He said you were a really good man. I should appreciate everything you've done for me."

I'd taken a bullet for him, and he was still disappointed in me. But then he threw a curve ball like this. I'd never wanted to be a son who lived for his father's approval, but that was exactly what I was doing. It somehow validated my sense of manhood...even though it shouldn't. I was a much better man than he was because I never would have risked my wife's safety in the first place. As I'd already proven, I took my wife's protection seriously. My father became arrogant in his capabilities and gambled something he couldn't afford to lose. "I've never heard him say anything like that to me...ever."

"I was surprised too. Caught me off guard for a second. There was a gun sitting on the counter between us, and four of his men had their palms resting on their guns. He'd just chased off the customers who had been drinking in the bar, but then he told me to go home to you... It was odd."

"Yeah..."

"Maybe he really is as straightforward as he seems. Maybe he does want to do the right thing for you by getting me home...but he also wants his revenge too. How can he want both at the same time? Beats me."

Losing his wife sparked a mental illness he could never recover from. He was far too gone—and he wasn't coming back. "I went to his house a few days ago. It's easy for me to get access to him. I walked right into the living room with a gun stuffed in the back of my jeans, but I didn't draw. I could have put a bullet in his brain, but I'd never pull the trigger. I tried once before and chickened out. Every time I see him, I chicken out again."

"You aren't chickening out."

My arms rested on my knees, and I stared at the floor.

"Not killing your father doesn't make you weak."

"But he's not my father." I lifted my chin to meet her gaze. Even though the topic of conversation was dreadful, it was nice to talk to her again. "He's another Kamikaze. He's another enemy I have to dispose of."

"But do you think he'd ever really hurt me? He had his chance but didn't take it."

That man was completely unpredictable. "I won't underestimate him. You're too valuable to make an assumption like that."

It was the first time her eyes had softened in an entire month. "That means you'll have to kill him."

He was the last parent I had, and putting him in the ground seemed so wrong. He was my father, the man who gave me his last name. My wealth and connections came from his lineage. Putting a bullet between his eyes felt so wrong—but he didn't give me another choice.

"Unless he has some kind of revelation."

"Not gonna happen."

"I don't know... He did try to patch us up."

That was a curve ball. "But he doesn't know what happened." I suspected if he did, his opinion wouldn't change. Arwen should still be grateful she had me to take care of her. She should be grateful she had her own wolf for protection.

"I suspect his response would be the same."

I rubbed my palms together before I leaned back in the chair. The gas fireplace emitted heat to the room, but it didn't provide the spark and crackle of real flames like my fireplace did. It was a much quieter ambiance, a new renovation this old house had needed. Even if we didn't say another word to each other, it was nice just to sit there together. Shadows of loneliness started to shroud me in depression. I'd never needed intimacy, but without Arwen, I was lost in the woods. I took it for granted when I shouldn't have, and now I was the only one to blame. I'd managed to earn the love of a beautiful woman, but I hadn't cherished it.

She turned her gaze on the fireplace and pulled her knees to her chest. It was almost ten in the evening, around the time when she used to fall asleep beside me. Her arms crossed over her chest, and she leaned her head back on the cushion of the couch.

With her gaze averted, I watched her. I watched the way her lips softened and parted slightly. I watched the way she tightened her clothing around her to keep warm even though I was right there. Her eyes grew heavy under the weight of fatigue, and that made her face more serene. When she was fired up and pissed about something, she was beautiful. But when she was subdued and calm like this...she was cute.

Cute wasn't in my vocabulary, so I didn't say it.

"I have a dinner party tomorrow. I'd like it if you came with me."

Her eyes flicked back to me, a little less tired than before. "You're the most social person I know."

"Not by choice."

"You always have a choice."

"It's good business practice." I stayed in touch with lots of wealthy people and kept my brand fresh in their minds. It added respect to my product, and people associated it in their minds with luxury. Bringing my beautiful wife only made me more appealing. Ever since she'd started to come around, my profits had nearly doubled. "Will you come?"

"I have a choice?"

I echoed her own words back to her. "You always have a choice."

"I'm not that interested in going to a dinner party...not after the last one. But I have to uphold my end of the bargain, right?"

She could do anything she wanted, and I would never kick her out. If she were smarter, she would have figured that out. I'd given her the freedom to do whatever she wanted the moment she became my wife. She had powers no one else would ever possess, but she was oblivious to it. "Right."

"Then I'll go. But I'm not performing a song—no matter how much they ask."

I'd have to talk to the host about it beforehand. Otherwise, the request would be made anyway. "I'll take care of it."

She turned her gaze back to the fire, her eyes growing heavy once more.

I'd been sleeping alone ever since I could remember, but now I struggled to get to sleep without her beside me. It'd been over a month since we were last together, but my mind still hadn't gotten used to the solitude. The bed felt too big now. "I'll let you get some sleep." I rose to my feet and walked to the door, knowing I would retreat to my cave and sleep alone. It was the longest I'd gone without getting laid, so my mind was in the gutter most of the time. There was nothing I wanted more than to peel off her leggings and push her knees to her chest so I could fuck her into the mattress. When we were together without a condom, I realized just how good sex could be. It had made my threesome even more anticlimactic. I traded in perfect sex with the perfect woman for something mediocre... It was my biggest regret.

She didn't turn around. "Good night."

I WALKED to her bedroom door and tapped my knuckles against the wood. "Ready to go?"

"I just need a minute."

I backed away and moved to the armchair in the hallway. This dinner party was more laid-back than the others, so I wore a casual suit and tie and had selected a cocktail dress for Arwen. My elbows hit the armrests, and my hands came together to rest. My fingers naturally moved closer together until they gripped the band of my ring. Absentmindedly, I fidgeted with the piece of jewelry. It quickly had turned into a habit, and anytime I found myself pondering anything, that was exactly what I did. The ring was still new to me and took time to get used to. The moment I put it on, I never took it off because that was how serious I was about this marriage. I wasn't just making it work for show anymore. I actually wanted to be married.

She opened the door and stepped out in a backless dress and ridiculous heels. Her hair was pulled up to show off her beautiful spine and the small muscles that flanked it on either side. Her pale skin was brighter in contrast to the gray fabric of the dress, making her fair skin look kissable.

I missed kissing her.

I rose to my feet and buttoned the front of my jacket, my eyes following her as she walked past me. My eyes took in the sight of her gorgeous figure and her perfect ass, and my cock ballooned to full mast in less than five seconds.

Damn.

She didn't look at me with the same lust. I'd shaved and worn a jacket that fit my strong shoulders well. Any other woman would at least give me a few seconds of her time. But Arwen acted like I wasn't there at all.

I caught up with her before she reached the stairs. "Here." I pulled her wedding ring out of my pocket and handed it to her.

She gripped the banister at the top of the stairs and looked down into my open palm. My jeweler had cleaned it and gave it an extra shine so she would be tempted to take it. A small hesitation came over her face, like she'd missed that ring for her own personal reasons. Then she turned away and headed down the stairs. "I'm not ready..."

THERE WERE ABOUT fifty people at the house, and I knew most of them. I hated sparking conversation with new people, but it was necessary for networking. Talking to people I already knew could also be boring. I lost either way.

But my wife shone like always, so she stole the show.

I walked into the main entryway and admired the painting on the wall. It was an original portrait of Christopher Columbus, just before he died in Spain. It was massive, taking up most of the large wall. I preferred historical art pieces because they were darker, more realistic. Modern art had pops of color that were borderline fantastical.

"Beautiful, right?" Sabrina sauntered to my side with a glass of scotch in her hand. She was a young widow. Her husband had passed away in a horrific car accident, and she was still shopping for a new husband.

"Yes." I didn't take my eyes off the painting.

"Your wife is pretty." She stood at my side, her fingers clutching the glass of scotch. With jet-black hair and green eyes, she was a beautiful woman. I'd be lying if I said I didn't notice—since I'd slept with her once. It wasn't long after her husband was gone that she'd wanted comfort and jumped into my bed.

"I know." I swirled my glass and took a drink.

She smiled. "I thought you said you would never get married."

She tried to dig her claws into me, but I didn't take the bait. She was already wealthy from her late husband's inheritance, but she still wanted more. She wanted to be a well-kept woman with a husband who ran the show. "Things change."

"Then you must really love her."

I continued to stare at the painting.

She pivoted her body toward mine, waiting for an answer that I would never give her. "Or do you?" Her hand moved to my arm.

My instincts kicked in, and I pulled my arm down, getting away from the soft touch of her delicate fingertips. "I'm not yours to touch, alright?" I turned my gaze on her, cold and unkind.

She brushed off the rejection with a slight smile then walked off.

Heels sounded a second later as Arwen entered the room, passing Sabrina on the way. Both women looked at each other, Sabrina smiling with her lips but not her eyes. She gave Arwen a glance-over before she kept walking.

Arwen came to my side. "What are you doing in here?"

"Admiring this painting."

"Did that woman admire it too?"

I lowered my glass and turned my gaze toward her. "Yes."

I knew her well enough to understand when she was jealous, and she was definitely jealous in that moment. Her eyes flashed in hostility, and with her superb intelligence, she could read a room so well. She must have felt the cold flame between two former lovers. She must have noticed the way Sabrina looked at me, caught a glimpse of her hand on my arm. Arwen had been smiling minutes ago, but now her lips were pressed tightly together in a frown.

I didn't make her ask for the information she wanted. "We hooked up a few times when her husband passed away."

She crossed her arms over her chest and stared at the wall. It was a priceless painting, worth tens of millions, but we didn't truly appreciate it. "She seems like she wants to hook up again..."

"No."

"People grab your arm like that often?"

I wanted to tell her there was no reason to be jealous, but I couldn't. I'd betrayed her trust. "When we were together, I told her I wasn't interested in marriage, so she moved on. I'm married now, so she feels a little stung."

"But you aren't really married..."

I didn't wear this ring on my left hand for looks or comfort. I wore it to show the world my commitment. "I *am* really married." I positioned myself in front of her, forcing her to look at me instead of the painting. "It doesn't matter if she wants me because I'm committed to you."

SHE REACHED THE SECOND LANDING, her perfect body shifting from left to right as she carried herself. In high heels and a dress that required perfect posture at all times, she handled herself with grace.

My eyes stared at her back until I reached the second floor.

She turned around to say goodbye, cutting me off from her bedroom. "Good night, Maverick."

I knew it would take time to fix the destruction I'd caused, but the wait was torture. It was worse when she wore a dress like that, the shape of her tits visible underneath the thin fabric. I wanted her on my bed, our naked bodies together, husband and wife. But Sabrina only made me look worse, so of course, Arwen was in a bad mood. "Arwen?"

She stopped and looked at me over her shoulder, her pose so perfect, it could be a painting.

With my hands in my pockets, I came closer to her, unsure what I would do once we were face-to-face once more. If I had full authority, I would grab her face and kiss her. But I had no power over this woman...none at all.

I moved into her body and slid my arm around her waist, my warm palm feeling the smooth glide of the curve of her back. The second my fingertips came into contact with her bare skin, I felt the small shock that exploded in my veins. It'd been so long since I'd touched her like this...felt her like she was mine.

She tensed at my touch but didn't pull away.

I secured my arm around her waist, and I pulled her close to me, desperate for the affection I'd once had access to on a daily basis. I could have hugged her whenever I wanted to, but I never took the time. Now, it was a luxury I couldn't have at my beck and call. I had to go for it and hope she wouldn't shove me off.

Thankfully, she didn't.

I kept her close and rested my chin on her forehead, my eyes closing like I might drift off to sleep. My other arm spanned across her back and reached for her other shoulder. Once she was against me, I tightened my hold just a little more. Her smell wrapped around me, taking me back in time to when she trusted me.

I missed when she trusted me.

She'd always had this look in her eyes...like I was the person she looked up to.

She rested her forehead against my chest. When she didn't pull away, I knew she wanted this too. She still missed me even though she was angry with me. She still lived for this kind of affection. Brandon had been a distraction for the night, just as the girls were to me. They didn't mean anything to either of us.

This did.

I kept my eyes closed and fantasized about lifting her into my arms and carrying her to bed. Vivid images of us kissing, touching, dropping clothes all over the floor came to me. I wanted to bend her over the bed and kiss the skin everywhere, devour her like a hungry wolf. I wanted to yank on her hair and use it as a leash to keep her obedient. I wanted us to be together, to go back to what we were.

But this was the most I would get.

I could hold on forever, but I knew I shouldn't. If I asked for too much, it would push her away. My arms slid down her back, and I let her go, hoping her scent would stay on my skin once my clothes were off. When the depression took me, I could just remember this embrace...and tell myself that I could still fix this.

"What was that for?" she asked, her fingers sliding past my arm until I left her touch.

If that wasn't obvious, she couldn't read me very well. "Because I miss you."

9
_____

ARWEN

By the time I got out of the shower, Brandon had blown up my phone with text messages.

Call me.

Did you move out of your apartment?

Are you alright?

Messages popped up every few minutes. When I'd left my apartment and returned to Maverick, I'd sent Brandon a cold text and said I was done seeing him. We were never serious, so I didn't feel the need to give a more detailed explanation.

He obviously didn't think I was serious.

I patted my hair dry with a towel then returned to the bathroom. I finished drying and styling my hair before I came back to the bedroom, a gray robe tied around my waist. When I glanced at my screen, I saw I had five missed calls.

I sat on the edge of the bed and picked up the phone.

A knock sounded on the door.

"Come in."

Maverick stepped inside. He was wearing tight jeans and a black blazer, the dark shadow on his jawline prominent because he'd skipped his shave that morning, but it brought out the color of his eyes.

My phone kept lighting up with text messages, but I ignored them.

He sat on the edge of the bed beside me, his arm brushing against mine. "Want to have dinner with me tonight?" After he'd hugged me in the hallway, he'd left me alone for a couple of days. He never pressed his advance too much. If he tried too hard, I would only step back.

I usually had meals in my bedroom, but I could go to the dining table for once. "Yeah, I'll meet you down there tonight."

"I meant we would go out to dinner. Take a drive to Florence."

Not once had we done that. The only time we'd had a meal outside the house was at one of his parties. But the two of us had never faced each other across a table in a restaurant.

The phone in my hand kept blowing up with more messages from Brandon. It became so frequent that I turned the phone to silent.

"That's not how you get rid of a guy." He grabbed the phone out of my hands and called him.

"What are you—"

"No, it's Maverick DeVille, Arwen's husband." He'd been soft-spoken just a moment ago, but he quickly fell into an aggressive role the second he felt threatened. "Your relationship with her is over. Call her again, and I'll kill you." He hung up and tossed the phone back at me.

Brandon must have taken the threat seriously because he didn't call or text again.

"How about that dinner?"

"How did you know that was him?"

"Because he's a man who lost you... I know exactly how that feels." He rose to his feet and turned around to look at me. "We'll leave at six. Wear something nice."

"Is this a social event?" Were we meeting another couple in the city? Meeting a few business associates?

"No. Just you and me."

HE SHIFTED gears as he accelerated to a higher speed. The road across the Tuscany countryside was abandoned and dark, like an open racetrack just for him. He sped his fancy car down the road even though we had all the time in the world.

If someone else were driving, I would grip the side handle and be terrified the entire way. But since Maverick was a man in control of everything, I wasn't afraid he would lose control of the wheel.

His watch reflected the lights from the dashboard, and the long sleeves of his blazer fit his muscular arms well. His slacks were tight in the right places, and with his recent haircut, he looked like a model waiting to be photographed.

It was strange seeing him wear that black ring all the time.

It was even stranger that I wasn't wearing mine. I constantly felt for my ring, absentmindedly fingering the spot even though it was gone. I'd worn it so long that it had become a part of who I was. Once I took it off, I'd felt a little lost. If I wasn't Mrs. DeVille, I didn't know who I was.

He entered the city and gave his car to the valet at the restaurant. His arm moved around my waist, and he escorted me inside, scoring a private table in the back without even having to give his name. It was a quiet restaurant, scattered with couples. Candles burned on every surface, making it the ideal place for romance.

I shed my coat and placed it over the back of the chair.

Maverick helped me sit down. He pushed in my chair then placed his palm on the back of my neck, sliding it under my hair. The touch was brief, only lasting a few seconds, but it was enough to make bumps emerge on my skin.

He moved across the table from me and took a seat. He got the waiter's attention right away and ordered a bottle of wine for us to share. He seemed to know exactly what he wanted without checking to see if they offered the particular bottle.

I picked up the menu and stared at the selections because I suddenly felt awkward sitting across from him. It was the first time we were face-to-face like this, sharing a meal like a normal couple.

We were anything but normal.

"How long are you going to look at that menu to avoid me?"

I kept looking just to be a smartass. "Until I find something good."

"The gnocchi is recommended."

"That does sound good…" I kept my head down. "What are you getting?"

"Whatever you're getting."

"That's boring." I finally set the menu down as the waiter approached and poured the wine. Just before he walked away,

Maverick grabbed the menus and handed them over. "We'll both have the gnocchi—and get these off the table."

The waiter walked away.

Now Maverick stared me down without restriction. "That's better."

The glow of the low-burning candles and the dim lighting in the room made it seem like the most romantic place in the city. All the couples were talking quietly over their dinners, some were young and had just discovered the heat of a new relationship, while others had veteran relationships that had deepened over time. But it was obvious that every single person in there was in love.

Me included.

Just looking at Maverick was enough to remind me why I fell for him in the first place. He was the strong and silent type, the kind of man that used actions rather than words. If something needed to be handled, he took care of it. He was a hard worker who ran his business with pride, and he treated his employees well. He was honest to anyone he encountered. And he was also selfless and brave. He'd hurt me so much, but I never felt unsafe with him.

Maverick held on to his glass of wine as he watched me, his brown eyes focused on me to the exclusion of everything else in the room. I was the only thing that mattered, the only woman who had his attention.

When Sabrina gave him a rubdown the other night, I immediately wanted to claim my property and chase her off. My unease disappeared when I remembered Maverick wouldn't reciprocate her advances even if he wanted to. There'd been lots of offers throughout the last few months, but he didn't take them. Only when things got real did he turn to someone else. It was no excuse for what he did...but I understood Maverick wasn't a two-timing liar.

That didn't mean I was ready to forgive him. I couldn't see that happening for a long time.

The silence continued, and it didn't seem like Maverick was in the mood to talk. He thrived in tense silence. It gave him the upper hand in every situation. He could tolerate the void that made everyone else uncomfortable. He swirled his glass then took a drink.

"How was work?"

He took his time getting the red liquid down his throat. "Same."

"Then how was your workout?"

He shrugged.

"You asked me to dinner, but you don't seem to want to talk."

"I don't want to talk about stuff like that."

"Alright...then what is there to talk about?"

"You."

"There's nothing interesting going on in my life...other than the fact that your father wants to kill me."

"You've been writing new music. How's that going?"

When I'd composed that song about him, it only took me thirty minutes to complete it. When I was emotionally charged, the words just flowed out of the pen and onto the paper. "Good. I've been writing a lot lately." I had a lot of material to cover.

"Have you ever thought of being a musician?"

"I already am."

"You're an opera singer. I meant, have you ever considered being a contemporary singer. Just you and the piano. I really think people would love it. I know the opera doesn't pay you much, so if you had your own production, maybe things would be different."

"I don't know...that sounds like a lot of work."

"It's not work if you love it, right?"

"I just meant doing both."

"You don't have to do both," he said. "You can quit the opera whenever you want."

Not everyone was rich like he was. "I can't quit. I need to work."

"But you don't." He leaned forward with his hand still wrapped around the stem of his glass. "You don't have to do anything you don't want to do. If you want to save your voice for your own act, that's a great idea. My money is your money. You're my wife—on and off paper."

I'd never used the money he gave me. I had debit and credit cards that he allowed me to have, but not once had I used them for anything. I cashed my checks from the opera and spent that on gas, clothes, and anything else I needed. Taking even a euro from him had never crossed my mind.

"Sheep."

I stopped ignoring his stare. "I asked you to stop calling me that."

"Well, I'm not going to. Listen to what I said." His left hand rested around the glass so his ring was always in view. Dark like charcoal and deep like his eyes, it was the perfect ring to suit his appearance. It was still strange to see him wear it...but it looked just right at the same time.

"I don't want your money."

"It doesn't matter if you don't want it. Legally, it's yours. If we really filed for divorce, you would have every right to take half of it."

"I'm aware." It would have been easy for me to demand half his estate because I was entitled to half his holdings. My love for Maverick had nothing to do with the assets he possessed, so therefore, I didn't want anything. I didn't touch anything that he'd worked so hard for. "I've never been interested in your money. You're the only thing I've ever been interested in."

His chest rose slightly as a deep breath entered it. His eyes softened as he let the air escape through his nostrils.

"I heard those two girls talking. I could see the dollar signs in their eyes. I could see the way they looked at you as some kind of sugar daddy. If you want a pretty girl who only cares about your money, mission accomplished. But I'm not one of those girls. I actually know you, Maverick. I like you...respect you."

His eyes filled with guilt.

"So, no, I don't want your money."

"I asked you to try. That's part of the deal."

"Why do you think I'm here?" I countered.

"I'm sorry I fucked things up, but I'm here now. I want this marriage to work. If I didn't, I would just shoot my dad and let you go out on your own. Even if he were dead, I still wouldn't want you to leave. I would want you to stay...because I want us to be together no matter what. I know I should have said this sooner and I shouldn't have screwed things up, but I'm fighting for you now."

It was impossible not to soften when he said things like that. Maverick DeVille was telling me he wanted to spend his life with me. He was basically asking me to be his wife. It was a marriage proposal...but a real one.

"You're my wife. What's mine is yours. I want to take care of you. I want to spoil you. I want to pay for your coffee and gas." He placed his hand over his chest. "I *want* to do those things."

He was just making it worse.

"Let me take care of you."

If this were two months ago, I would completely let go and give him what he wanted. I would rely on him completely, allow him to give me the world. But now that he'd hurt me, I was scared to accept those kinds of gifts. "All I really want is you, Maverick. We should work on our relationship before we talk about things like that. I can't let you take care of me when I don't trust you. Trust takes time...sometimes a really long time."

His eyes shifted down to his wineglass as he swallowed his disappointment. He pulled the glass closer to him and stared at the table, his face somehow more handsome when he was brooding. "I've got all the time in the world."

WE SAT in silence the entire drive home.

It was a long trip just for dinner, especially when we had a private chef at the house. It was our first official date, and Maverick had probably wanted to make it special.

One hand stayed on the wheel, while the other rested on the gear shift. When he drove fifteen minutes without shifting, he could pull his hand away, but he left it there like he hoped I would grab it.

I craved affection, but I wasn't ready to pretend nothing had happened. If we were really going to make this marriage work, then I would have to forgive him eventually. But even if I did forgive him, that didn't mean the trust would come with it.

He parked the car in the driveway, and we entered the house. It was quiet because Abigail had gone to bed. It just started to sprinkle when we walked up the stairs, the large windows showing the falling rain outside.

Christmas was just two weeks away.

It had slipped my mind.

We walked up the stairs to the second landing.

Maverick turned to me and immediately locked his arms around my body, holding me just as he did a couple days ago. His hold was aggressive, like he'd been counting down the minutes until he could hold me again. His arms rested in the curve of my back, and he brought me as close as he could.

I let it happen because I was too weak. I couldn't fight it, not when it felt like home.

His hand slid under my hair, and he held the back of my neck. His head angled down so he could look at me, press his forehead against mine as he held me at the top of the stairs. His eyes moved to my lips, the longing evident.

He shouldn't bother kissing me. I wouldn't let it happen. The last person he kissed was one of the stupid bimbos that came over. I hated to think about kissing the same lips they'd kissed. They used to be mine...until he gave them to someone else.

Maverick was smart and didn't try. "Thank you for having dinner with me."

"Thank you for taking me."

His fingers continued to caress my hair as he held me, the storm getting louder outside. Winter was a cloak of gray, dreary and dead. It brought water to the soil and mud to the surface. It was my least favorite season, but trying to stay warm with Maverick made it a little better.

It would be nice to invite him to bed, to have a strong man sleeping beside me. Sharing my space with Maverick became a luxury I never had before. My lovers slept over, but I'd never had a man like him. Now I missed it.

But not enough to give him an invitation.

"Goodnight." I pulled away.

"Arwen."

I turned back around but didn't touch him again. It didn't matter how handsome he looked in that outfit or how much I missed that hard body underneath those clothes. It was too soon to pretend everything was okay.

He pulled a folded piece of paper out of his pocket. "Just so you know..."

I took it from his hand but didn't understand what it meant. I unfolded it and recognized all the labs that were ordered for a typical STD panel. Everything was negative. I folded it again, but if he expected me to be touched by what I'd seen, he was stupid. "A bit presumptuous?"

"I just want you to know you have the option." He slipped his hands into the pockets of his jeans. "I'm not going anywhere. I'm not going to be with anyone but you. So, whenever you're ready... I'm ready too. Just the two of us. I promise."

When we were together, I'd been eager for this conversation, for the moment when we would really cut out all other lovers. Condoms would be dispensed with because they would be unnecessary. It was just the two of us...and we wouldn't be separated by anything. We'd only made love that way a couple of times, and they were the best nights of my life. I wanted to have them again...just not now.

Maverick gave me a slight nod before he turned around and headed up the stairs. He probably hoped something would happen tonight. If he'd been celibate like he promised, it must have felt like an eternity.

But no, I wasn't ready.

We weren't ready.

THE WINTER SEASON brought inhospitable weather, so there was nothing to do but stay indoors. I couldn't use the pool or jog around the grounds because we were in the middle of a storm. So, I did something unexpected—I went to the gym.

I'd just reached the hallway when Maverick stepped out of the double French doors. In just his sweatpants and workout shoes, he had a streak of sweat on his bare chest that shone under the lights. It was the same way he looked during sex, hot, sweaty, and pumping with blood. A towel was over his shoulder.

When he crossed my path in the hallway, he looked over my outfit. "Is this a dream?" he teased.

I smacked his arm playfully. "I'm bored, and there's nothing to do outside. The weather is too crazy to go anywhere. So, I thought I would walk on the treadmill or something." When my eyes glanced up his body, I noticed my ring sitting on a chain around his neck. I stared at it for a couple of seconds and wondered how long he'd been wearing it.

"So the only way to get you to exercise is through boredom?"

"I guess..."

He gave a slight smile, his pretty eyes lighting up. "You know, there are other ways to exercise..." He brushed his arm against mine as he walked by, pulling off the comment when no one else would have been able to.

"I prefer doing it alone."

He stopped and turned around, his eyebrow cocked at my choice of words.

"You know what I mean..."

"Yes. But I'm going to pretend I don't."

WHEN IT FINALLY STOPPED RAINING, I headed to Florence before my performance and went shopping. Christmas was just around the corner, and I wanted to pick up a few things for Abigail and the servants.

I also wanted to get something for Maverick.

He was a difficult man to shop for, being as he already owned anything he could possibly want. He had a three-story estate and only used the second floor for the gym. The rest were guest bedrooms that were never filled.

Sometimes I wondered why he lived there at all. It was too big for one person.

Well...I technically lived there too.

I didn't have a lot of money like Maverick, so I couldn't afford the designer stuff he usually wore, but I found a shirt that would look great on him. The color of Bordeaux wine, it was a collared shirt that would suit his large frame. He would never wear it to a fancy event, but maybe he would wear it around the house. It was still steep for my budget, but I got it anyway. If he didn't like it, I could wear it with a belt and some leggings.

I went to the theater and prepared for my performance. After a wardrobe change and new makeup, I went on stage, sang my heart out, and then finished the show. As much as I loved being a singer, the repetitive nature of the job had started to wear me down. It wasn't good for my vocal cords either. The director wanted to use me more often than the understudy, but that meant I had to sing three times a week...which was a lot of work on my throat. Sometimes I wondered if I should take Maverick's suggestion and just do my own thing. But that would force me to rely on him completely, financially. If that were the case, I wouldn't have even been able to buy his Christmas present on my own.

I was pulling the pins out of my hair, deep in thought, when Brandon approached me from behind. "Uh...what are you doing?" I turned around in my chair and stared at him blankly, relieved Maverick wasn't there to put a gun to his head.

"Your husband picked up the phone, and we never got a chance to talk."

I got to my feet, my eyebrow cocked like he was crazy. "Brandon, I ended things with you a while ago."

"Through text," he snapped. "We never really talked about what went wrong. You didn't even give me a real chance."

"Brandon, nothing went wrong. I just got back together with my husband."

"But do you *want* to be with him?" he asked. "Because it doesn't—"

"Yes." I didn't think twice about my answer, and that was scary. Even after what he did, I knew he was the man I wanted to be with. My heart ignored his faults because it only cared about his positive qualities. I saw so much of the good and not enough of the bad. I was already getting soft for him once more, and we hadn't even spent much time together. I drove to the city early just to get him a Christmas present when I didn't have to do a damn thing. "Brandon, I'm sorry if I hurt you, but I was clear about what our relationship was."

"You aren't wearing your ring—"

"Because she doesn't need to wear it." Low and threatening, Maverick's terrifying voice fell across our shoulders like a heavy fog. In a black suit with combed hair, he owned the backstage with his presence, murder in his eyes. His shoes tapped against the wood as he slowly came closer. "She's still my wife." He stopped in front of Brandon and stared him down hard, his eyes steady with violence. "She's mine—not yours. Now, run."

Brandon turned his gaze back on me.

I stopped him before he said anything stupid. "Run." Maverick wouldn't be patient for long.

Brandon made the right decision and walked away.

Maverick watched him go without turning his head. His eyes followed Brandon until he left the area and returned to the auditorium. In his hand was a single red rose, and he set it on my dressing table. "For you."

"You didn't need to threaten him like that—"

"He's lucky I didn't kill him. I'm a man of my word. Luckily for him, I'm not today." He stepped closer to me, his black ring matching his attire. The wedding ring was so sexy on him. It was a fantasy, seeing him as a devoted husband...especially when I was his wife. "If he bothers you again, I will kill him. Let's just hope he finally gets the hint."

"He will."

He picked up the rose and held it out to me.

I brought it to my nose and smelled it. The scent of rain overcame my senses. "Thank you."

"You were wonderful tonight. You're always wonderful."

I placed the rose back on the table. When I returned in a couple of days, it would be wilted. But it was difficult for me to throw away anything Maverick gave me. It was the reason I'd worn my wedding ring for weeks after I'd left. It just felt wrong to take it off. I wondered if it was hanging on a chain underneath his clothes at that very moment.

"Can I take you home?"

"My car is here."

"My guys will drive it back."

"Oh...then, yes."

He noticed my bags sitting beside my table. "Are these yours?"

"Yeah, I picked up a few things for Abigail and the girls..."

He picked them up and carried them for me. "Would you like my jacket?"

"No. I have mine." I grabbed it off the back of the chair and pushed my arms through the sleeves.

He held the bags with one hand and helped me.

It immediately reminded me of the way my father would help me put on my coat. He did it when I was a child, and even when I became an adult, he still did the same thing...always helping me.

We suddenly felt like a married couple, like a husband and wife going home after a long day. My throat tightened when I realized how comfortable it was, how much I wanted it. When my jacket was secure, I faced him again.

"What's wrong?"

"Nothing...I'm just not looking forward to walking in the rain." Our wedding day had been such a painful event, but Maverick had made it as bearable as possible. He'd taken my hand and guided me the entire way, helping us navigate the lie so everyone would believe it was true. He'd been guiding me all along...since the moment we met. He was the one who'd entered my apartment and convinced me to marry him. If I didn't, I would die. And marrying him was the best thing that had ever happened to me.

Love couldn't be contained or controlled. It couldn't be shoved in a can with a lid on top. Since it was ever-growing, it was always getting bigger, always filling the space with pressure until the lid popped off. That was how it'd been with us since day one. It was a slow burn, hatred turning to dislike, and dislike turning to admiration.

Maverick kept watching me, noting the way my eyes changed. "It feels right to me too."

HE CARRIED my bags into my bedroom and set them on the coffee table. "You've got a lot of stuff here."

"I got Abigail a box of chocolates and a couple of bracelets I found at my favorite boutique. I never see her go out, so maybe this will give her a reason to get dressed up." I picked up the bags and placed them in my closet so Maverick wouldn't spot the collared shirt.

"That was nice of you." He slid his hands into his pockets, and he looked like a powerhouse in that suit. With a clean jawline and a masculine face, he already looked handsome even without a designer suit tailored to fit him perfectly. All the things that others needed to be presentable were unnecessary for someone like him. He already carried himself like a leader, like the most admired man in the country.

It was hard to believe he was mine...if I wanted him to be. "She does so much for me. I thought she deserved a nice Christmas. Do you get your servants anything?"

"I give them jobs, don't I?"

I pressed my lips together tightly and forced back the smile that came to my mouth. It was a predictable answer and fit him so well. I slipped off my jacket and hung it in the closet before I came back to him. My fingers flicked on the fireplace because I was cold the second my shoulders were free of the warm jacket.

He glanced at my appearance in the tight dress. The look was subtle and quick, but it was still noticeable at the same time. He kept his hands in his pockets and his shoulders straight, eyes trained on me.

I waited for him to walk out. "Thanks for the ride home."

"My pleasure. I've got to keep the dogs away."

"That was the only reason you came?"

He shook his head slightly. "I came to see you. That was the only reason."

I stopped a few feet in front of him and crossed my arms over my chest. The more I felt the pull between us, the more I tried to fight it. Maverick had done a terrible thing, and I didn't want to forgive him so quickly. He really hurt me, and it wouldn't be right to sweep it under the rug...but my heart wanted something else. With every passing day, I missed his bedroom more and more. I wanted to be the recipient of his amazing kiss, be the woman under him in the throes of passion. I wanted to be his wife.

Maverick waited patiently, like something might happen. If I were willing, he would slide his hand under my hair and kiss me as every piece of clothing dropped to the floor. His desperation was palpable, his desire filling the air around him. It'd been over a month since he'd last gotten action, but he remained faithful to me because I was the only woman he wanted.

It was going to happen anyway, so I may as well go for it.

But I couldn't bring myself to do it. "Goodnight, Maverick."

His eyes fell in disappointment, and a quiet breath escaped his nostrils. Like he was a deflated balloon, his shoulders slowly sagged and his chin tilted toward the ground. "I can't last much longer…"

"What's that supposed to mean?" Was he giving me an ultimatum?

"It doesn't mean anything." He stepped closer to me, his hands sliding out of his pockets. "When I watch you sing, it turns me on like crazy. Your voice…your mouth…everything. Then when it's just us two, all I can think about is how beautiful you are, that you're my wife and no one else's. There's nothing in this world that turns me on more. I could be with another woman, but that would be unsatisfying. I could be with myself, and that would be a letdown too. I'd rather just keep waiting…even though it's driving me mad in the process."

My arms tightened over my chest, like they were a protective barrier that could actually stop him.

Maverick read my body language with disappointment. He bowed his head slightly then turned to step out of the room. "Goodnight." He headed to the door without looking back. His expansive shoulders looked beautiful in his jacket, and his narrow hips led to a tight ass. It couldn't be seen directly, but the tug of the fabric made it obvious.

I watched him go without asking him to stay.

But I missed him the second he was gone.

10
_____

MAVERICK

CHARLES AND I TALKED ABOUT BUSINESS AT HIS HOUSE. WE HAD A few rounds of scotch and a couple appetizers, but we spent most of our time discussing his needs for his businesses. He had a few restaurants across Europe, not just Italy, and fulfilling his need for my exclusive product wasn't as easy it seemed. Our wheels weren't produced by machines because the process was far too delicate. It required a hands-on approach, which made it expensive, and also difficult.

"You're asking for a lot—but I'll do my best." This business was a family legacy. Handed down through the generations on my father's side, it was a great source of pride for the DeVille family. The food industry wasn't that interesting to me, but my family's hard work through generations to achieve this kind of success was fascinating. It made me feel connected to my grandfather and my great-grandfather...and even my own father.

"Excellent." Charles shook my hand as he guided me to the front door.

Juliet escorted Sabrina to the front door at the same time. They must have gotten together since Charles was busy with another meeting. The second Sabrina saw me, her eyes lit up like this was a turn of events that she wanted.

I shook hands with Charles then kissed his wife on the cheek. "Thank you for the scotch. It was very smooth."

Sabrina said goodbye as well, and when she noticed me step out the door to leave without her, she said, "Maverick, would you be a gentleman and walk me to my car?"

The asshole inside me wanted to tell her to fuck off. It's what I would have said to someone else. But that would be a poor way to start my new business relationship with Charles. "Of course."

Sabrina finished saying goodbye then wrapped her coat around her body. She walked out with me, keeping so close to me we looked like lovers to anyone who noticed us. Charles had a place in the city, so we stepped out onto the sidewalk and headed to our cars a street over. It was quiet because it had rained just hours ago. The sidewalk and street were damp with the recent rainfall. It was actually slightly less chilly because of the blanket of clouds overhead.

Her heels tapped against the concrete as we walked together. She kept her jacket tight around her to cover the sleeveless dress she wore. "You two have fun?"

"Money is always fun." I was in dark jeans with a leather jacket. House calls between men weren't meant for suits. Neither one of us cared unless it was a formal dinner party.

"Juliet and I are planning a charity dinner in a couple of weeks. Just ironing out the details."

"I'm sure it'll be lovely." We turned the corner and approached the line of cars at the curb. "Which is yours?"

"The white Maserati."

I escorted her to the driver's door, knowing Sabrina would try something since she'd asked me to walk her to her car. She didn't care about her safety. She just wanted attention. She couldn't have me anymore, so she wanted me more—even though I was married.

She turned around and leaned against the door, having no intention of getting inside. She smiled slightly, her dark lipstick outlining the prominent curve of her lips. "I have a place just down the street."

"As do I."

"Then which one is closer?"

I'd never cared about matrimony or fidelity. Lots of men I knew had affairs on a regular basis. I'd never had an opinion about it because it didn't matter. I'd never wanted to get married because monogamy was too cruel for even a short period of time. Lying and sneaking around weren't my game. But now...I felt completely different about it. If you were married, you made a promise to someone, and you shouldn't break that promise. It disgusted me that Sabrina saw the wedding ring on my left hand but didn't care. She saw my wife with her own eyes but still didn't care. Losing her husband made her numb to everyone else's pain. "Sabrina, I'm married."

"So is everyone else."

"I'm not like everyone else." My wife was at home, clueless to the conversation I was having at that very moment. If she knew, she would be livid. But when I came home, she would continue to be angry with me and ignore me. I was committed to a woman who still couldn't forgive me for what I'd done. I was so damn hard up from my celibacy, and she would never know if I fucked Sabrina at my apartment. But that was not the man I wanted to be. I wanted to go home to my wife and be with her...because she was the only woman I wanted anyway. "Goodnight, Sabrina."

Her hand reached out and grabbed me by the arm. "If you're playing hard to get, it's working."

I twisted out of her grasp and stared at her coldly. "Touch me again, and I'll break your hand."

When the game was over, her eyes started to smolder with offense. Her playfulness evaporated, and she was left with the cold sting of rejection. When she invited a married man to bed, not a single one said no...until now.

I walked off and left her behind.

"I'm cutting you off." Kent grabbed my glass and pulled it away. "You're gonna crash into a brick building if you keep this up."

"I'm fine." I drank like I had an indestructible liver. Booze never slowed me down, and even when I had too much to drink, I was in control of my faculties. Most of the time, people couldn't even tell I'd been drinking.

"Trust me, you look like shit." He kept the glass out of my reach. "I might have to call your wife to come get you."

"Don't get her involved in this."

"I think she'd like to know you're totally shit-faced."

"I'm not her problem." After I walked away from Sabrina, Kent and I met up for a drink. He flirted with a few women, but he stuck to my side and didn't leave with a buddy for the night.

"She's pissed at you. Doesn't mean she stopped caring about you."

"She should stop caring about me..." Now that Kent noted my stupor, I did feel drunk. My eyes weighed as much as bowling balls, and I had to think about my words before they emerged from my mouth.

"Sabrina just threw herself at you, and you said no. You're a good guy, Maverick."

I scoffed. "If I were a good guy, I wouldn't have fucked things up to begin with."

"I understand why she's angry, but don't be so hard on yourself. You've done a lot for that woman, and now that you're ready to be in a real relationship, you're the most loyal guy in the world. She needs to let this go."

"You think so?" I reached for my glass again.

He pushed it farther away. "Nice try, asshole. And yes, I think she does. This relationship didn't start on good terms. It's taken a while to find your stride." He grabbed my phone off the counter.

"What are you doing?"

He scrolled through my phone book and found her number. "Getting your wife to pick you up."

"Why don't you just take me home?"

"I'm not driving all the way out there. Forget that shit." He held the phone against his ear.

"She's probably asleep—"

Her voice was audible when she answered. "Maverick, everything okay?" Like always, her voice sounded like music.

"This is Kent. We met a while ago. Your husband is totally trashed and needs a ride home."

"Is he alright?" she asked.

"He's fine," Kent said. "Won't throw up. But he definitely can't drive."

"Thanks for letting me know," she said. "I'll come get him."

Kent hung up and set the phone on the counter.

"You asshole. I'm trying to fix this relationship, and you tattle on me? She's gonna see me at my worst."

"That's what marriage is, asshole. You're there for each other through the good and the bad."

"I'm supposed to be there for her...not the other way around."

He took a drink of his scotch, even though it was torture for me. "That's your problem, Maverick. You think everyone deserves everything...but you don't deserve anything. That's exactly how you got yourself into this mess. You'd think you'd learn..."

WHEN SHE GOT THERE thirty minutes later, the alcohol had soaked into my blood and hit me a little harder. I sat at the counter and did my best to seem normal, but the room was starting to spin.

"She's here, man."

I didn't embarrass easily, but I was humiliated that she had to see me like this.

She came to my side, her hand moving to my back. "Got carried away, huh?"

I stared at the counter.

"He's a bit shy right now." Kent helped me to my feet and placed my arm over his shoulder so she could suspend my weight.

I almost pushed him off because of my pride, but once I realized how unbalanced I was, I used him as a crutch.

Kent guided me outside and to the black BMW at the curb. "He got shit-faced pretty hard tonight."

"I've never seen him look like this before." She followed behind us.

Kent opened the passenger door and helped me into the seat. He even buckled my safety belt before he shut the door.

I rested my head against the leather and closed my eyes, my thoughts in hyperactive mode. My chest felt tight from all the alcohol. My blood was boiling from the heat. My blood alcohol level must be astronomical.

"Why did he take it so far tonight?" Her muffled voice came from outside the car.

"I think he's just stressed."

"About what?"

"Well, Sabrina threw herself at him again. Invited him back to her apartment. Obviously, he said no."

Fuck you, Kent.

"Oh..." Her beautiful voice was weak.

"I know it's none of my business, but Maverick is a good guy, and he feels like shit for what he did. He's in this relationship now... Cut him some slack. He's done a lot for you. He's trying to be what you deserve. Trust me, this guy gets ass handed to him like change, and he hasn't taken any offers. Just let it go."

If I weren't so drunk right now, I'd punch him in the face.

Arwen didn't respond to his comment. "I should get him home. Thanks for calling me." She got into the car a second later and started the engine.

I looked out the window and noticed it had just started to rain. I didn't have the courage to look her in the eye and thank her for coming to get me. I didn't want to face her at all, not after what

Kent said to her. Like a coward, I closed my eyes and pretended I
didn't hear anything at all.

I WOKE up when we returned to the house then made the labo-
rious journey to my bedroom.

"You want me to call for help?" she asked as she walked
beside me.

I did my best to walk perfectly straight, to pretend I wasn't drunk
out of my mind. My movements were slow, and my steps weren't
full of purpose. My chin was tilted toward the ground because
looking up caused the room to spin. "No."

I reached the staircase and held on to the banister—because I
had no choice.

Arwen stayed beside me with her hand resting on my back. She
walked with me slowly, keeping my pace without rushing me.

It took an eternity to get to the top floor.

Why did I decide to have my bedroom all the way at the top?

We reached the hallway, and my muscles relaxed now that we
were so close. I didn't throw up on the ornate rug or trip down the
stairs. I made it into my bedroom and started to peel off my
clothes. Somehow, I got stuck in my jacket, unable to pull my arm
out of the material. It seemed like I was tangled in a pile of ropes.

"Here." Arwen grabbed my jacket and got me loose. She folded it
then placed it over the back of the chair.

My t-shirt was easy, so that was a simple process. I got my jeans
undone and pushed them off. My shoes were kicked off, and I
didn't think before I pushed my boxers down too. I was so drunk
that I didn't want any piece of clothing on me at all.

"Um..."

I made it to the bed then collapsed on top, the world spinning now that my physical orientation was different. My body stretched out across the mattress, and I didn't get under the sheets because I'd felt so warm in my clothes. A headache was pulsing at my temples, and my entire body felt like it got hit by a semi.

Arwen sat at the edge of the bed then slid her fingers into my hair. Soft and delicate fingertips grazed across my forehead and deep into my scalp. Once her touch glided to the back of my head, she massaged my skull and released the pressure from my headache. "Can I get you anything?"

I opened my eyes and looked at her above me, her hair messy because she got out of bed to pick me up. She didn't wear makeup and her jeans and t-shirt were plain, but she was a million times prettier than Sabrina would ever be. "No."

"How about some painkillers?"

"I'm fine..."

She opened my nightstand and found a bottle of pills. She must have noticed all the condoms were cleaned out of my drawer because she paused to look inside for an instant. There was already a glass of water that Abigail brought when she did the turn-down service in my room. "I know you just want to sleep, but you should be proactive about this. I have a feeling you've never been hungover before."

I was hungover all the time. It just didn't affect me that much.

"Come on." She guided me to sit up.

I grabbed the pills and shoved them into my mouth before I downed the water to wash them down. I returned to the bed once again, my body softening in defeat.

Arwen pulled down the sheets and got me tucked into bed. She placed the covers up to my stomach before she opened my dresser and pulled out a t-shirt.

"I'm too hot to wear anything…"

"It's not for you." She changed out of her clothes and prepared to pull the shirt over her head.

I didn't care how drunk I was; I was going to look. I turned my gaze on her, but my vision was blurry. I couldn't make out anything except the hazy outline of her curves.

She came back to me then got underneath the covers.

Was she really going to sleep with me? Was this all I had to do to get her into bed?

She got comfortable beside me then ran her fingers through my hair again.

I felt like shit, but I also felt so damn good. This woman was rubbing me, lying with me, and looking after me. Her affection surrounded me, made me feel like I'd fallen backward in time. I closed my eyes and ignored the migraine, choosing to cherish this moment.

"I thought I had to get you to stop smoking. Now I have to get you to stop drinking too."

"I'll never drink this much again."

"Good…now I don't have to kick your ass when you feel better."

Her words brought a smile to my lips. I reached for her impulsively and tugged her against my frame, wrapping our bodies tightly around each other. I hiked her leg over my hip and buried my face in her neck. It was better than sex because it was more intimate. It meant so much more than a good lay. If I got to

choose between the two, I would have picked this every time...
even though I couldn't have sex anyway.

She let me hold her. A moment later, her fingertips returned to
my hair.

"Sheep...I miss you." I closed my eyes and felt myself drift away.
My arms were locked around her body, and I would never let go. I
used to have this every single night until I threw it away. Now that
I had it again...I wouldn't let it slip through my fingertips.

"I miss you too..."

11

ARWEN

I took the breakfast tray from Abigail. "Thank you."

"Is he awake?"

"No. He's knocked out cold. But maybe when he smells the coffee, he'll open his eyes."

"Let me know if there's anything I can do."

I returned to the bedroom and set the tray on the table. It was full of pastries, coffee, fresh fruit, and two hard-boiled eggs.

Maverick was still in bed, dead asleep even though it was almost eleven. He hadn't moved from his spot since he fell asleep last night. When I got out of bed, I had to fight for my freedom from his grip.

I walked to the bed and looked down at him, his face a major improvement compared to the night before. It wasn't so sunken and pale. Life and vitality were slowly returning to his skin, giving it a healthy color. The alcohol was destructive to his system, and once it'd been metabolized, he finally came back to life.

I sat beside him and ran my fingers through his hair.

My touch caused him to take a deep breath and slowly wake up from his drunken stupor. His eyes opened slowly, and he took in the sight of my face for several seconds before he registered what he was looking at. His fingers rubbed the sleep from his eyes, and he groaned like he just got hit by a truck. "Fuck, I feel worse than I did last night..."

"No. You're just sober now, so you can actually feel it." My fingers continued to caress his hair, gently coaxing him back into reality.

"Then maybe I need a drink..."

"How about coffee instead?" I filled a mug then set it on his nightstand.

He slowly pushed himself up and rubbed his sleepy eyes again. His hand reached for the coffee absentmindedly, floating in midair, until I guided him where it was supposed to go. He lifted the mug and brought it to his lips. "Smells good." He took a couple of sips before he set it down again.

I'd slept by his side, getting the best night of sleep I'd gotten in a while. His bed was just as comfortable as I remembered—and his touch was even better. When Kent told me about Maverick's night, I was jealous some beautiful woman wanted to get in his pants so bad...and I was also touched that he didn't cave. He wasn't getting sex from me, but he didn't look for it elsewhere. If he really wanted to be with another woman, he could easily hide it from me. He seemed serious about this relationship now... unlike before.

"I'm sorry you had to drive out there and pick me up. I'm embarrassed by the whole thing..." He didn't look me in the eye as he made his confession, so it seemed like he meant every word. He was an innately confident man, but underneath that hard shell was a vulnerable soul. "I would have called one of my men if I were thinking clearly."

"I didn't mind getting you, Maverick. I'm just happy you didn't drive home."

"I probably would have walked to my apartment instead."

"I have a feeling you wouldn't have made it that far...or remembered where it was."

He rubbed his temple as he chuckled. "Yeah...guess not. And Kent is a jerk-off that would have left me there."

"I doubt it. He did call me."

"I would have preferred it if he took me home himself."

"I wouldn't."

He dropped his smile and tilted his gaze back to mine. Although foggy with a hangover, Maverick's clear mind was still there.

"I didn't mind picking you up, Maverick. I'm your wife. It's my job to take care of you."

Anytime he received unconditional affection, he immediately shifted away like it disgusted him. He was incapable of being the recipient of something good, of receiving something rather than giving it. He looked away, right on cue. But then he had a change of heart and looked back at me once more.

"I want to take care of you."

His chest rose with the big breath he took, but he kept his gaze focused on mine. He didn't brush it off like all the other times. After a slight nod, he whispered, "Thank you."

It was the first time I saw a change in Maverick. Sometimes he hovered between being a good man and an asshole, but this was the first time he'd taken a definitive step toward a different life. He crossed a line that could never be uncrossed. He made a gesture he'd never made before.

My hand moved to his, and I gave it a gentle squeeze, my heart releasing the deadly toxins it had absorbed from his malice. Now, it seemed like things were really different, like we were a team.

His hand squeezed mine in return. "I didn't throw up, right?"

"No. You don't remember?"

"I remember you picking me up but not much else."

"Why were you drinking so much, anyway?"

"It was a long day. I had a lot of work to do at the office, and then I met Charles in the city. Whenever I meet anybody, there's always a lot of drinking involved. Then I met up with Kent at a bar...and that was a terrible idea. I'm a heavy drinker who handles my liquor well. Never really crossed that line before. But somehow, it happened last night. When I hit my threshold, it was too late... I was long gone."

"I think you need to sober up for a week to give your liver a break."

"Yeah...I'm sick of scotch anyway."

"Wow, you really must have learned your lesson."

"Of course I did," he said. "The whole thing is embarrassing. How can a man take care of his wife if he's so drunk, he can't take care of himself?"

"Because he's a human being who can make mistakes too. Relationships aren't one-dimensional. It's about giving and taking. It was one of the few times you needed me, and I was glad I could be there for you. You've done so much for me..." He'd saved my life multiple times and became the rock underneath my feet. He supported me in every way possible, from cradling my heart to holding my hand.

"But I was happy to do those things."

"I know."

He grabbed his coffee again and took another drink. "First time I've had breakfast in bed. Abigail must have known it was bad."

"She knows you pretty well." I watched him drink, watched his throat tighten and shift as he let the warm liquid fall into his stomach. He drank half of it before he returned it to the tray. "So...Sabrina wanted to jump your bones?"

Maverick looked across the room, his eyes settling on the flames that burned in the fireplace. "Did you start this?"

"Yes."

"That's impressive. Logs are pretty heavy."

"And I'm pretty strong. Don't change the subject."

He grinned slightly but still avoided my gaze. "What do you want me to say?"

"The truth."

"Yes...she wanted to sleep with me. Now, what's for breakfast?"

I'd hated that woman the moment I saw her touch my husband on the arm. It was obvious she was a seducer the second I looked at her. She fished for affection from all the men around her, wanting their obsession because it kicked up her validation. She'd already slept with Maverick, but she wanted him more— just because she couldn't have him. "Is that her type? Married men?"

He shrugged. "I think she prefers powerful men with fat wallets."

"Well, this powerful man and his fat wallet are taken."

He turned his gaze back to me, a ghost of a smile on his lips. "Yes...they are." He looked into my eyes, his brown eyes shifting back and forth as he watched jealousy turn into annoyance.

When I got like this, I was easy to read. "She lost her husband years ago, and she's been shopping for a replacement."

"Then she needs to stick to bachelors."

"She wants the best of the best. Their marital status doesn't matter."

"That's disgusting."

"Most men have affairs. It's not that surprising."

There was nothing less attractive in a man. Sneaking around and lying about his whereabouts to have a mistress made him less of a man. At least Maverick was up front about his intentions. Now he seemed to be a truly devoted husband. He wore his wedding ring everywhere he went and carried my ring on a chain. I could see it now, lying against his bare chest. "You aren't like that…"

"No, I'm not." He grabbed my hand again and rested it on his lap. "And I will be faithful every day for the rest of my life. Not because I'm bound to be, but because I want to be. I could be crazy drunk, and I still wouldn't do it."

My anger toward him was fading more and more. Evaporating like water on a summer day, my temper was slowly dissipating. That anger was being replaced by affection at an equal rate. I didn't want us to be divided any longer. I wanted us to try to be husband and wife…to give this a real shot.

"Please." He pulled me closer to him, bringing our faces close together. "You said you would try. Please try for me."

He was the most irresistible first thing in the morning like this, with tousled hair and a sleepy gaze. His tight frame was so warm and inviting. His strong body looked even sexier when my wedding ring hung down his chest, like he was carrying a torch for me. My arm circled around his waist, and I pressed my face into his neck. "Okay…I will."

"Wow...that is a big-ass Christmas tree." At the bottom of the stairs in the entryway, the tree extended all the way to the second floor. It had to be at least twenty feet tall. Decorated with ornaments in gold and white, it was a beautiful piece for the house.

Maverick came down the stairs dressed for work. "Yeah. It'll be great for the party."

"Party?"

"I'm having a Christmas party here. Thought it would be a good way to make a lasting impression before springtime."

"I thought you didn't do parties."

He shrugged. "It's part of business."

"Well, I'm looking forward to it."

"Good. I need you." He stood beside me and examined the ornaments, his eyes lifting up to see every foot of it. It'd been a day since he woke up with a migraine, and he was finally getting back to his usual schedule. Cutting out the booze gave him an extra boost of energy. "Want to have dinner with me tonight?"

"Not out of the house."

He turned his gaze back to me, his eyebrow raised.

"It's supposed to rain tonight. I'd rather stay home."

Once he understood I wasn't blowing him off, he looked at the tree again. "It seems like it's always raining."

"Yeah...I hate winter."

"I should head to work. I'll see you later." He turned toward me, like he might give me a kiss goodbye. Instead, I got a slight smile and an affectionate look. Then he walked off, his ass perfect in his jeans.

Even though the rift had been healed between us, nothing had changed. He didn't try to make our relationship physical, and neither did I. It was the first time I'd said I would actually try... I just didn't know what that meant.

MAVERICK HAD WATER WITH DINNER. Booze seemed to be temporarily gone from his life at the moment. He sat across from me and didn't blink an eye over the red wine I had with the dinner Abigail supplied.

"How long have you known Kent?"

He shook his head slightly. "I can't even remember. Almost ten years, I guess."

"Was he at our wedding?"

"Yeah."

"I don't remember seeing him."

"There were so many people there. You probably did meet him but just don't remember."

"Is he your best friend?"

He shrugged. "I don't identify with that term. But he is my closest friend...if that's what you're asking." He finished his food and left his half-eaten plate on the table. A green salad with fish and vegetables had been our dinner.

I ate all of mine because everything Abigail made was delicious. I liked my food simple but flavorful, and she did an excellent job of constructing that. It wasn't packed with extra oils and spices until it was heavy and overwhelming.

Now that my walls were down, things were starting to feel the way they used to. We were friends who could talk about anything together. Conversations rolled off the tongue easily, and it was relaxed.

I'd missed it.

When we finished dinner, we made our way upstairs to the second landing.

My heart started to race because I knew something was going to happen. It'd been a long time since we'd been together, and it was obvious he was anxious. I was anxious too. I'd been sleeping with Brandon for a while, but that wasn't as passionate and satisfying as it was with Maverick. It didn't compare, actually.

When we reached the second landing, Maverick did the unexpected. He turned to me, one hand in the pocket of his jeans, and dismissed me. "Goodnight, Arwen."

He didn't try to kiss me. He didn't dig his hand into my hair and pull me close. He didn't kiss the back of my neck like a hungry wolf wanting to rip me to shreds. It was so unexpected that all I could do was stare.

He walked to the foot of the next set of stairs. "My previous offer still stands. If you want me, you know where to find me." He walked up the stairs and disappeared from my sight. His footsteps grew quieter until they were completely silent.

I'd expected him to chase me, to pin me up against the wall and take me. I'd expected the wolf to come for me, to claim me as his own the way he used to. But I remembered all the times I'd rejected his affection. He took my hand and asked for my forgiveness so many times, but my answer was always the same. He couldn't read my mind now. He couldn't know what I wanted. I didn't even know what I wanted until he walked away.

I headed upstairs to his bedroom and let myself inside.

His jacket and shirt were over the back of the chair, and his jeans were left on the floor where Abigail would pick them up in the morning. The bed was empty, so he was in the bathroom, probably brushing his teeth and washing his face.

When he heard me enter his space, he stepped back inside. He was barefoot and in just his boxers, his tanned skin contrasting against the chain around his neck. My diamond ring immediately reflected the low-burning flames in the hearth. Little rainbows cast across the wall.

He stopped and looked at me, watching me enter his bedroom.

I was the one making all the decisions now. I came to his bedroom because I wanted him...whatever that might mean. Jumping into bed with him again seemed premature, but there was nowhere else in the world I'd rather be. I didn't want to sit in my bedroom alone and blankly watch TV. I wanted to be there...with him.

Tall, muscular, and so handsome that I couldn't blame Sabrina, he stared at me. His boxers hung low on his hips, the prominent sex lines of his hips making a noticeable V. His stomach was tight with his eight-pack, something no amount of booze could erase. The man stayed in perfect shape no matter what came his way. His brown eyes were welcoming like a cup of coffee in the morning, the perfect temperature to chase away the frost.

I crossed the distance between us and moved closer into him, watching the way he stared at me in anticipation. It was unlike him to be so docile, but perhaps he was scared making a move would only push me away. My heart beat like a drum, my palms turning sweaty even though it was raining outside. A fire burned in the fireplace, the crackling sound matching the heat underneath my skin. I stopped in front of him, my eyes level with his chest. My old ring twinkled at me, like it was winking. This was hidden underneath his clothing everywhere he went, including the night when Sabrina tried to steal him away. Why wouldn't she want him? He had it all—looks, money, and respect.

My hands moved to his muscular arms, and I pressed into the warm skin. The dips between the different grooves were so prominent, so unmistakable. I could feel the power hum under his skin like a distant melody. I lifted my gaze then rose onto my tiptoes, bringing our faces closer together.

When my intentions were clear as a blue sky, his arm hugged my waist while his free hand slid into my hair just the way I liked. His fingers dug deep, wrapping around the strands like he was using it as a rope. He pulled me tighter, letting me feel just how hard he was in his boxers.

I rested my forehead against his and appreciated the surge of affection that burned in between us. The chemistry was hot like an erupting volcano, my hormones burning like they were on fire. I could feel his chest rise and fall, sense the labor of his breaths. His desire matched mine, hot and fiery.

I missed this.

I'd never had this with anyone else. Not Dante. Not Brandon. Not anyone.

His hand slid to the back of my neck, his fingers possessive. "My sheep…" His thumb brushed across my cheek. He looked at my mouth like he was claiming it with his gaze. His arm tightened a little harder, and he turned into the wolf I remembered. Authoritative and powerful, he took control of me like it was the most natural thing to do, like he'd been waiting all his life to do it.

I didn't want Sabrina or someone else to have him. I wanted him all to myself. "I never want to share you again…"

His eyes shifted back and forth as they looked into mine. With just the simplest expressions, he said so much. His fingers tightened even more. "You never have to."

"I never want you to hurt me again."

"Never." His hand moved up my back and pulled me into him as he kissed me. With open lips and a slight growl, he felt my lips with his own and gave a gentle suck. He breathed quietly as he felt the burn between our mouths. The first touch was the slowest, was the longest. His hand cradled the back of my head, and he released an anxious breath.

I could feel the pleasure in his veins, feel the passion in his touch. He'd been waiting for that kiss as long as I had. He'd been looking forward to this like it was the most important thing in the world.

He kissed me again...and again.

His hand was in my hair, and his arm tugged me against his chest. His kisses were mixed with heavy breaths, pants of desire. Open. Close. Kiss. Suck. Lick. Repeat. He tugged on my bottom lip with his teeth before he released me, only to do it again a second later. His tongue swiped against mine before another warm breath filled my lungs.

No one could kiss like Maverick DeVille.

His cock throbbed against my stomach, the large girth twitching noticeably. It seemed to swell longer and thicker as our kiss continued, the crown noticeably enlarged. He wanted to break free of his bottoms so he could get to me as quickly as possible.

I didn't expect sex when I walked through the door. I just wanted something from him...anything. But now my fingers pushed his boxers down over his muscled ass so his cock could come free.

His hands immediately pulled my shirt over my head then unclasped my bra. When I was in just my jeans with my tits bare, he palmed one tit and flicked his thumb over the hard nipple. His lips rested against mine, but he didn't kiss me, focusing on the way I felt in his grasp.

I sucked in a deep breath every time his thumb felt me, every time my nipples pebbled just a little harder.

His other hand grasped my other tit, and he moaned. Like a teenager feeling up a girl for the first time, he thoroughly enjoyed it. His strong fingers kneaded my tits aggressively, palming and claiming each one of them. His anxious breaths fell across my skin as he continued to feel me up. With an aroused expression, he looked into my face as he watched my reaction, watched me come apart under his touch.

A man had never touched me this way before. A man had never been so confident in his embrace, had hands that could stroke a woman so perfectly. He glanced at my lips then my eyes, watching me bite my bottom lip as I arched my back, pressing my tits farther into his hold.

My hand reached for his dick, and I gripped it in my fingers. It felt like a pipe running with hot water. It was hard as steel and hot like steam. I felt the grooves along the edge of his crown, the pulsing vein protruding from his shaft. My thumb swiped across the hot skin as I squeezed him in my grasp.

He twitched every time I gave him a squeeze.

His hands dropped from my tits and unfastened my jeans. He pushed them over my ass then lowered himself to his knees, his mouth kissing the valley between my tits. His tongue tasted me as he pulled my pants and panties down to my ankles. Just like the wolf that he was, he started to eat me. His kisses turned aggressive, accompanied by deep growls. His hands palmed my cheeks, and he lowered his kisses to my belly. Kissing me everywhere and squeezing me into him, he enjoyed me like it was all for him.

The chain hung around his neck, the ring tapping against my body as he moved.

Any doubt I had disappeared the instant he kissed me. I didn't think about the two women who had slept in the bed that belonged to me. I didn't think about the resentment and the pain. Now it felt like just the two of us, husband and wife.

He rose to his feet and scooped me up at the same time, cradling me in his arms and holding me flush against him. He was so strong that carrying a full-grown woman was no problem. His hands gripped my ass as he held me against his chest. My legs were open to his torso, my wet pussy pressing against his warm skin.

He carried me to the edge of the bed but didn't lay me down. His lips found mine, and he kissed me again, this time slow and passionate. His lips caressed mine like he had all the time in the world, like sliding into my body wasn't the highlight of his night. He sucked my bottom lip then breathed into me, a sexy moan coming from that masculine throat.

My nails scratched his back then dug into his hair. My ankles were locked together around his waist, and my feet could feel the flames from the hearth behind him. My ankles dug into him a little deeper as the kiss continued. I pulled at his soft strands and never wanted to share him with anyone else ever. I never wanted to sleep with another man. For me, this was all I wanted. I'd never directly told Maverick that I loved him because he wasn't ready to hear it, but when he was ready, he was the only man I wanted to share those words with. He was the only man I wanted to father my children, to be my husband until we were old and gray.

He rolled me onto my back and moved on top of me at the same time, his narrow hips fitting perfectly between my thighs. His heavy weight caused the mattress to dip and my body sank underneath him. It'd been so long since we'd been together that I forgot how perfect it was, how well we fit together.

His cock pressed against my clit and became slathered in my moisture so easily. With a slight tilt of his hips, he smeared his base with my arousal and became coated in the lubrication. Drops leaked from his tip and dripped onto my stomach, sticky and warm. His arms anchored behind my knees, and he held himself on top of me, the hunt still in his eyes. Now that we were naked together, he didn't hold back. He claimed his prize like he'd earned it.

He grabbed his base and pointed his head at my entrance. After a quick thrust, he pushed past my tightness and slowly sank deep inside, stretching me to capacity as he pressed deeper and deeper.

My nails dug into his arms, and I took a deep breath as I felt his large dick claim me. He was bigger than Brandon, bigger than any other man I'd been with. It felt so right when we were together...especially without a barrier separating us.

When he was balls deep, he closed his eyes and moaned. His forehead rested against mine, and he breathed through the pleasure, his cock twitching now that it'd been reunited with the one place where it wanted to be. "Jesus Christ..." He slightly rocked his hips, testing the slickness and the tightness.

My fingers felt the definition of his arms, the way his muscles swelled under his tanned skin. I could feel the power of his physique, the way he held his beautiful body so effortlessly on top of me. He enjoyed me like he forgot how good a woman felt. Like there'd been no one else before me who mattered, I was the only person he would actually remember.

He was already a sexy man who looked handsome with any expression he gave, but he looked particularly delicious on top of me. With his mouth clenched tightly and his body rigid with pleasure, he was the sexiest man I'd ever seen. He opened his eyes and looked at me once he realized this was real, that he'd finally gotten me back.

My fingers slid past his cheek and into his hair as I pulled him close to me. I was stuffed full of his length, stretched so wide apart, I couldn't take anymore. It'd been so long since we'd been together that I forgot how good it felt...and how painful it was too. I brought his face close to mine and kissed him.

My ring rested against my chest between my tits, shifting up and down with his movements. The metal was cold to the touch in the beginning, but as the air heated up between us, the metal turned warm and inviting.

He kept his pace slow and kissed me at the same time, his long length delving deep inside then pulling out to my entrance. He pushed all the way in once more, taking a deep breath as he plunged so far. Moans escaped his mouth as he thrust inside me. His pace always stayed the same, even and slow.

My fingers clutched his hair, and I kept him close as my body melted into a puddle. All my nights had been spent alone, remembering how good this used to be. Now that it was happening again, I could hardly believe it. I could hardly believe that my memory had been so clear...because it was exactly the same.

He kissed me harder as he rocked his hips and pushed deep inside me. Slowly, he moved, giving me all of him every single time. He breathed hard, and his body became coated with sweat as he worked to please me, as he brought us both into euphoria.

Now that I had this back in my life, I never wanted to lose it again. Sex wasn't this good with just anybody. It was only amazing when it was with the right person. Despite the rocky relationship we had, I knew this was where we were both supposed to be. We were supposed to be together...just like this.

12

MAVERICK

It was the best night of sleep I'd ever gotten.

The trials of my life had finally passed, and everything was in order once more. There shouldn't be a random woman beside me every night, a face and name I would easily forget. It should only be one person.

My wife.

When I opened my eyes, I found her next to me. With her hair a mess and her soft skin peeking out from under the sheets, she was a living angel. Her blue eyes were hidden behind her lids, but knowing they were there made her angelic. With sleep still heavy in my eyes, I watched her for a bit, content to see her lying there.

She inhaled a deep breath then stretched her legs, like a cat waking up from its nap.

It was the first time I'd gone to bed fully satisfied. I'd tried jerking off a couple of times, but it never left me feeling so full. It was always a hollow release, a painful reminder that I couldn't have what I really wanted. But I spent the night buried inside the same woman over and over. With nothing in between us, I filled her with load after load...washing away any trace of Brandon and making her mine.

My life was finally back to normal.

It felt so good.

I had a long day ahead of me, but I chose to ignore responsibility and stare at her instead. It'd been a long time since she'd been in that bed with me, not counting the night I was drunk out of my mind. I hadn't been sober enough to really enjoy her presence at the time.

Now I could.

The backs of my fingers brushed up against her skin. Soft like a rose petal and smelling just like a new blossom, she was as beautiful as a porcelain doll. She had the attitude of a mule but the beauty of a goddess. That made her even more appealing to me.

She woke up moments later, her beautiful eyes taking me in with restful laziness. She stared for a couple of seconds before her curved lips spread into a smile. She closed her eyes once more then reached her hand for my side. Slowly, she brushed her fingertips against me, feeling the outline of my muscles. "Morning, Wolf."

"Morning, Sheep." I moved over her and placed a kiss on her forehead. Her sexy figure was draped in the sheets, hugging her beautiful curves and barely covering her perky tits. She turned to me for protection and guidance, relying on me as the one person who could keep her safe. It inflated my ego...and made me feel like the luckiest bastard alive.

She propped herself on her elbow then ran her fingers through her hair, being sexy without even trying. She kicked off the sheets slightly and revealed the top half of her body, her sexy tits and hard nipples. She scooted closer to me then wrapped her arm around my stomach. Her head moved to my shoulder, and she sighed in relaxation.

My arm circled her waist, and I kept her anchored to me.

"I'll never get out of bed…"

"That's fine with me."

"But I need to eat…drink…and pee."

"I think you can make it."

She chuckled into my shoulder. "Do you have work today?"

"I always have work. I also need to prepare for that party."

"That's right. That should be fun."

I wasn't much for socializing. All I cared about was getting respect for my family name and earning some cash.

"A Christmas party…there will be lots of champagne, decorations, and cheese."

"Yes, lots of cheese."

"I'm excited." She leaned into me and kissed me on the mouth. "I'll have to find something to wear." She scooted out of bed and prepared to get her day started.

I grabbed her by the wrist and dragged her back into the bed. "You can find something to wear later." I moved between her legs and smothered her back into the mattress. "For now, you're still mine."

———

ABIGAIL RAN over the list of everything she would have for the party. "Is there anything else you wanted?"

"No. Looks like you've already taken care of everything." I smoked my cigar behind the desk, the rain pounding against the windows behind me. A winter storm had arrived, but it was expected to clear just before the party. "As always."

She folded up her list. "Forgive me for asking, but would you like me to invite your father?"

Abigail and I never discussed personal matters, but since she shared occupancy of my estate, she was aware of everything that happened on the premises. She knew my father and I didn't see eye to eye. She probably had no idea my father wanted to kill Arwen, but it was better if she didn't know that piece of information. "No." Even if we were on speaking terms, I doubt he would have wanted to come anyway. He used to be social when my mother was alive, but now that she was gone, he had absolutely no reason to show his face anywhere.

Abigail didn't blink an eye over my answer. "Alright. Need anything?"

"No."

She let herself out.

With my cigar between my teeth, I turned back to my laptop and took care of business. Running a cheese company wasn't as interesting as my involvement in the underworld had been, but at least it was simple. I had a wife now, and I wouldn't make my father's mistakes by living a life of adrenaline. It wasn't worth it— no matter how much money was on the table.

A few minutes later, Arwen walked inside. Carrying an article of clothing covered by a white plastic bag, she seemed to have found the dress she would be wearing that evening. She was all smiles and joy as she walked in, but when she noticed the cigar in my mouth, her eyes changed to two pits of burning hell. She threw the dress over the back of the couch. "Want me to slap you?"

I pulled the cigar out of my mouth and let the smoke rise from my nostrils. "It's pretty hot...I wouldn't mind it."

She stomped to the desk and snatched the burning cigar out of my hand. She smashed it into the black ashtray, pounding it unnecessarily hard like this was really personal. It turned into mashed potatoes right under her fingertips. "If you want me to be your wife, then this has to go."

"Are you going to hold that over my head every time you want something?"

She didn't blink. "Yes."

I smiled slightly. "How about a compromise? I'll do it once in a while—"

"No. You're quitting here and now. Or I walk."

I rubbed my fingers across my jawline, the scent of smoke still on my fingertips. This woman could coerce me into doing anything because she had all the power. Just like a tyrant, she knew she could do whatever she wanted—so she did. "Alright."

"I mean it. If I catch you with a cigar again, I'm gone."

I just got her back, and I wasn't losing her again. I opened my top drawer and pulled out the box of cigars sitting there. I pushed them toward her, throwing in the towel for good.

She eyed the eight untouched cigars then looked at me again. "I want your promise, Maverick. You're a man of your word."

I gave a slight nod. "Alright...I promise."

She grabbed the box and tossed it in the garbage.

I felt a slight pang of sadness when I watched them fall to the bottom of the can. Good cigars gone to waste. It was like watching my former life disappear, watching bachelorhood become a memory. All the things I used to love were no longer important. I shed my former life and took on a whole new role.

Wasn't as scary as it used to be.

She came back to the desk with her hands on her hips, as if she expected me to argue with the law she'd just laid down.

It was a small sacrifice, so I didn't complain.

She grabbed the dress hanging over the back of the chair and pulled off the plastic cover. Underneath was a pastel blue dress that reminded me of a winter wonderland. With subtle sparkles in the material, it seemed like it was filled with small ice crystals. It was low cut in the front which was great for her awesome rack, and it flared out along the waist and reached down to her feet. "What do you think?"

"I'm not big on fashion, but I can tell that will look stunning on you."

She held it up to her frame and smiled. "Thank you."

With some diamonds around her throat and on her wrist, she would like the perfect queen—and I was her king.

She returned it to the bag to keep it clean and safe. "Is there anything you need me to do to help out?"

"No."

"Do you want me to play any music?"

I was certain everyone would expect it, especially in my home. It would be nice to have her sit at a grand piano near the Christmas tree and fill the halls with her beautiful song. Even if she sang a song about her undying love for me, I would hang on to every word. "Only if you want to."

She smiled. "If it makes you happy, then I want to."

I wanted to listen to her beautiful voice fill my home all the time. It brought life into this house, chased away the darkness that slowly crept into every crack and corner. Painful memories filled this entire place...but slowly she erased every single one. "I always want you to."

THE SEX WAS BETTER than I remembered.

All my other fuck-a-thons felt hollow and unsatisfying. Sometimes it seemed like I was doing it just to do it...even if I didn't like it. I didn't know what else to do with myself. Sometimes I wanted to prove a point...but I had no one to prove it to.

Sex with my wife was the best I'd ever had.

I didn't want to be a monogamous man hard up for a single woman. I didn't want the commitment, the mediocre fidelity. But I was happiest with Arwen. I was definitely more satisfied. I could be alone and continue to make a point...but who would care about any of the points I tried to make?

This was where I wanted to be.

This was the woman I wanted to be with.

She crawled on the bed and got on top of me, buck naked with her hair framing her perfect tits. Her eyes sparkled like flecks of gold in the sand as it washed up onshore. She lowered herself on top of me, her soft and warm skin rubbing against mine.

With my back to the headboard, I slid my hand up her gorgeous legs until I gripped her cheeks. I felt the tight muscle under my fingertips as I stared at her firm tits. She was so beautiful that my cock couldn't stop twitching.

I'd never seen anyone more beautiful in my life.

Why would I want someone else when I could have the most desirable woman on the planet?

Marrying her began as a chore...but it became the best thing that ever happened to me.

Her hands pressed against my chest, and she palmed my muscles, feeling how hard my frame was. She rocked her hips slightly, grinding her wet pussy over my hard length. She was a good lover, letting me take the reins but occasionally taking them herself. She ground a little harder then moaned, getting off on how hard my dick was.

Now I appreciated her attributes even more. I appreciated her petite shoulders, her perfectly proportioned tits, her slender belly, and her sexy hips. She was stunning from head to toe—and she was all mine.

I unclasped the chain from around my throat and slid the ring into my palm. The diamond had been hanging there for a long time, accompanying me everywhere I went. It was on me during my shower, underneath my shirt while I worked out at the gym. It was part of me now, a vigil for the woman who shared my name.

She looked down and watched me handle the ring.

I grabbed her left hand and started to slide it on.

But she pulled away. Her hand left my hold, and her fingers contracted into a fist, denying my advance in the most brutal way possible. That ring had sat on her finger for so long, but now she had no connection to it anymore. "I'm sorry... I'm just not ready."

The ring stayed between my fingertips as the anger rushed through me. Just when it seemed like everything was okay between us, she stabbed me in the gut when I wasn't paying attention. My fingers tightened around the ring, but then I forced my body to relax. I was the reason all of this happened in the first place. I hurt her...and it would take a long time to fix everything I'd broken.

I swallowed my pride and my anger and returned the ring to the chain.

"You don't need to keep wearing it..."

"I want to." I clasped the necklace around my throat and let the ring tap against my chest a couple of times before it stilled. Now the moment between us was ruined by the offer I made, by the rejection she so easily issued. Just when I thought our past was really behind us, I was reminded that she was still hurt by what I'd done. I needed to be more patient. I needed to make her feel secure in this relationship, that I wasn't going to turn cold if things became too serious again.

She stayed on my lap and watched me with apology in her eyes. She probably felt just as shitty rejecting me as I did being rejected. Her eyes moved down to my chest, and her hands rested at her sides. She was still in my lap, but the electricity between us was long gone.

I'd been so eager to be inside her, but now all of that heat vanished. I was reminded of how I let her down, how I was an unfaithful husband. I'd never questioned my own worth, but when it came to Arwen, I didn't feel good enough.

I slid her off my lap then walked into the bathroom. I'd already showered that morning, but I turned on the water and got inside. The warm water flattened my hair, and the steam fogged the glass. Drops of water ran down the tiled walls, and the heat made me forget it was raining outside. Something about a hot shower could clear my thoughts better than booze and cigars. Noise was canceled out by the falling water, so it made it easy for me to ignore the world around me. I closed my eyes as the water washed my thoughts away.

The door opened and closed behind me.

I didn't open my eyes because I knew exactly who it was. She could have returned to her bedroom and given me the space I needed... But I didn't really want space. I wanted us to be what we used to be, even though that seemed impossible. I opened my eyes and turned around.

Her hair immediately flattened with the humidity, and her skin glistened from the steam. Her tits tightened against her chest as her nipples pebbled in the heat. She moved closer to me, her chin lifting to meet my gaze as she drew closer. "I still want you..." Her hand moved to the center of my chest as she stepped under the water and let her strands stick to her wet skin. Her makeup started to run under the water, but I liked the way it began to drip. It reminded me of her tears, when her eyes would glisten because her climax was too much to take.

I wouldn't turn down a beautiful woman in my shower, so I disregarded her earlier rejection and felt my body come to life with desire. My cock inflated to full mast and started to ooze from the tip. Now that this woman was mine again, I wanted to be inside her always. I wanted sex every night and every morning. I was a married man, and I wanted to enjoy it as much as possible...especially when I was married to a woman like her.

I cornered her against the wall then hiked her leg over my hip. With the water running down us both, I pressed her into the warm tile and sealed my mouth over hers. Moans echoed in the small enclosure, but were soon swallowed by the falling water. I hiked her leg a little higher and rubbed the base of my dick against her anxious pussy. With just the right pressure, I could make her shudder, make her wince from a mixture of pleasure and pain.

She held on to my shoulders and kissed my anxious lips, her tits dragging against my chest as we moved together. She was suffocated in my arms, crushed between the tile wall and my heavy body. Her deep breaths turned to moans, and soon she was fisting my hair in desperation.

My hand guided my crown past her tight entrance, and I slowly sank inside, feeling a warmth that was even better than the hot shower. I moved farther into her until my length was happily sheathed, surrounded by her heavenly slickness. I hadn't fucked a pussy like this all my life, and now there was no going back.

This was all I wanted. It was the best cut of meat, the best flower on the vine, the best everything. Why would I want to settle for second best when I had the first-place winner right here? My cock claimed it as a permanent home.

Her nails scratched down my back as she felt me, her eyes glistening with moisture instantly. Her head rolled back, and she bit her bottom lip. "Maverick..." She said my name in the sexiest way with that angelic voice. She turned a single word into a beautiful song instantly.

My arm scooped under her leg and kept it pinned up as I thrust deep inside her, my dick wanting to venture farther and farther even though there was nowhere left to go. Whenever I fucked this woman, I always had to have her as deeply as possible, to enjoy every single inch of that perfect pussy.

One hand went to my ass, and she tugged me into her, taking my large size bravely. Even when it hurt her a bit, she continued to push through, savoring the pleasure and denying the pain. She kept biting her bottom lip over and over just to stop herself from screaming.

My arms picked her up completely, and I pinned her against the wall, letting my ass work to fuck her hard in place. I sank in deep with every stroke, drove my cock as far as it would go before I pulled out once more. I breathed hard against her mouth as I felt all the muscles in my body tighten from desire. Sex never fatigued me. It felt so good that it spurred me on indefinitely. I wanted to keep going forever...and never wanted to stop.

WE LAY side by side in bed, the flames in the hearth dying out until there was nothing left behind but hot embers. The only light came from the crack under the door into the bathroom. Sex in the shower led to sex on the bed, making the sheets damp because we didn't bother to dry off in between.

Now, we lay there, silent.

She turned on her side and looked at me, her hair damp and messy across the pillow. "Can I ask you something?"

"Anything."

"Be careful what you wish for..."

"I have nothing to hide." She already knew my greatest crimes and my worst flaws. There was nothing I could say or do to lower her opinion of me.

"Alright...am I the only woman you've been with without a condom?"

I was expecting a more philosophical question, especially when the answer to her question was so obvious. "Yes."

"Really?"

"Would I lie?" With one arm propped under my head, I glanced at her face then looked at the ceiling again.

"No...but I'm surprised."

"Why?"

"You're in your thirties."

"I don't see why age has anything to do with it. I'm a wealthy man from a noble bloodline. A woman might say she's on the pill, when in reality, she wants to trap me in a hold I can't escape. I always wear a condom—no exceptions."

"Then what about me?"

"You're an exception."

"You just said no exceptions."

"You're special. You're my wife."

A slow smile crept onto her lips, affection burning in her eyes. "I do feel special."

"Have you been with a man like that before?"

She nodded. "A few."

Disappointment rushed through me, but it was a stupid feeling to have. She was a beautiful woman who had men dying to be her one and only. Of course, they wanted to be monogamous and committed to her.

"But I like it the most with you." Her hand snaked across the bed to mine. "It feels so good when you're inside me...when I can feel you when you aren't there anymore. It's hot and heavy."

This was turning me on all over again. "You like my come, Sheep?" I scooted closer to her on the bed, wrapping our bodies around each other. I hooked my arm around her back and pulled her deep into me, practically making us a single person.

"Yes."

I rested my forehead against hers and closed my eyes. The peaceful feeling that washed over me was unlike anything I'd ever felt before. It was more potent than any drugs I could take. It was serene, divine. She made my brain shut down so the darkness couldn't get into the crevices of my mind. She made me feel complete...like there was nothing else I needed.

KENT CAME up to my side, looking dapper in a suit and tie. He already had a glass of champagne in his hand as he admired the enormous Christmas tree in the entryway. The string quartet played music for everyone to hear. "Wow...this place is nice." He whistled under his breath.

"Are you wearing a suit?" I asked, mildly surprised.

He brushed his hand over his shoulder. "Yes. And I look good in it."

"Didn't realize you owned one."

"Shut up. I don't want to punch you at your own party."

"And I don't want to stab you so close to Christmas."

He took a drink of his champagne then examined the crowd of people mingling. Dressed in ball gowns and suits with booze in their bellies, they somehow enjoyed the festivities and didn't grow tired of them.

This party had barely started, and I was already tired of it.

"Where's Mrs. DeVille?"

I shrugged. "Sweeping someone off their feet, I suppose."

"You two getting along?"

We were fucking a lot. So, yes. "Things are better."

"She still wanted to be married to you after your drunken episode?"

Not only did she still want to be with me, but she also took care of me. She was there the entire time even though she could have handed off my care to Abigail. She ran her fingers through my hair and watched over me the whole night. "I guess so."

"Hold on to her, Maverick. Not too many women will stay around after that shitshow." His eyes surveyed the crowd.

"Did I even invite you to this?" Abigail sent out invitations weeks ago, but I was certain Kent's name hadn't been in the pile.

"Yes. At the bar."

"When I got so drunk I couldn't remember anything?"

"Yep. I thought I could pick up a fancy lady for the evening."

"Most of them are married."

"Most," he emphasized. "But not all. And marriage is just a piece of paper... Who cares?"

My eyes narrowed on his face as the offense went straight to my heart. I imagined Kent making a move on Arwen when I wasn't in the room. Even with a wedding ring on her left hand as a sign of her commitment, he still thought it was appropriate to test the waters. It bothered me all the way down to my core. "It's not just a piece of paper. It's a lot more than that..."

He turned his gaze back to me, his lips rising in a smile. "It is, huh?"

"Yes."

"So, things are going well with the missus, then? Lots of fucking?"

After we were together again the first time, it happened nonstop. Every night we were making the headboard tap against the wall, and every morning we were having quick fucks before we started our day. I'd confide those details to him if Arwen were just a random woman...but she was my wife. "There's a widow here named Sabrina. She's your type."

"Widow?" he asked. "Is she old?"

"My age."

"Oh…a lonely young woman. That sounds exactly like my type."

"She was the woman who hit on me a couple of weeks ago."

"Gotcha." He nodded slightly. "So, she's definitely down to get nasty."

"She likes rich men. I'm not sure if you're rich enough."

"I may not be a billionaire like you, but I've got plenty to offer." His eyes moved across the room and stopped when he noticed something. "Damn, is that your wife in the blue dress?"

My eyes followed his gaze. She stood in a blue gown with slender straps over her shoulders. With a deep cut in the front that accentuated her perfect rack, she looked like a princess living in my castle. Her brown hair was pulled back, and the gown trailed to the floor, fitting her curves so well. She stood out from everyone else because she was so gorgeous. "Yes…the one and only."

Kent whistled again. "No wonder you put on that ridiculous wedding ring."

Ever since it slipped over my knuckle, it hadn't come off. Now I was used to wearing it all the time. The weight suited me, and the color suited me even more. "I put it on because I'm married."

He chuckled. "And it looks like you're happily married."

"Yeah…I think I am." I watched her talk to people whose names I couldn't even remember. It seemed like she was the host of the party because she walked up to everyone and made them all feel welcome. She'd never been particularly funny, but she managed to make people laugh so easily.

"I guess if I were married to that woman, I'd be happy too."

"Well, you aren't," I said darkly. "Don't forget it."

He nudged me gently in the side. "Don't worry, I know she's off-limits. No fooling around with your friend's sister, mother, ex, and the woman he loves."

"You forgot wife."

"Woman you love...same thing."

13

ARWEN

I recognized Sabrina from a mile away. In a tight black dress and a smile so fake, she was obnoxious just to look at. The woman preyed after my husband like he was available for solicitation.

No, bitch. He was mine.

But I took the high road and ignored her. It would only give her more satisfaction to know she got under my skin. Maverick didn't fall for her seduction, so there was no reason to be threatened by her.

I just wished he hadn't invited her.

"Okay, don't tell Maverick I told you this." Kent appeared at my side, looking a little different because he wore a three-piece suit and had his hair combed back. "But you look so damn hot tonight."

"I definitely won't tell him that." He'd smash his glass against Kent's skull and make a huge scene in the middle of the party. "He'd lose his temper so fast. And thank you."

"You're welcome." He clinked his glass against mine. "Do you find these parties as dull as I do?"

"They aren't so bad. I've met a lot of interesting people through Maverick."

"If you want to meet interesting people, go to a strip club."

I rolled my eyes. "You and Maverick are nothing alike. I'm not sure how you're friends."

"That's where you're wrong. We are alike. Well...we used to be. Things have changed for him. He used to be the shit-talking asshole that I am now. Ever since he met you, he's mellowed out a lot. No more strip clubs. No more women in general. He's become the pussy-whipped husband he vowed he would never be."

"He's not pussy-whipped."

"Trust me, he is. That guy loves you."

That was a scary word for us. The second Maverick received my devotion, things got ugly. "Did he say that to you...?"

"No, but it's obvious. I've watched him stare at women for ten years. Not once has he ever looked at them the way he looks at you."

I lowered my gaze, touched by what he said.

"The guy wouldn't be playing house like this unless he wanted to. That's the biggest indicator right there. Wearing his wedding ring everywhere he goes...turning down easy pussy...a man is only like that for one specific reason. You're that specific reason."

Maybe his mistake should stay in the past where it belonged. It was obvious things were different now...very different.

"So, can you point me in the direction of Sabrina? I hear she's hot."

I'd rather her dig her claws into Kent than my husband. "She's standing over there...in the black dress. She's got dark hair."

Kent scanned the crowd until his eyes locked on his target. "Damn, she's sexy. Alright, this party just got better." He finished off his drink then handed me the empty glass before he walked off to get a date for the evening.

It was the first time I'd had a few seconds to myself. I'd been chitchatting since the first person walked inside, and now I got to catch my breath as I carried the empty glass to a passing waiter. Most of the time, people wanted to talk about my performance at the opera or music in general. Very rarely did people actually ask me about the cheese business, which was good because I really knew nothing about it. Maybe I should be more involved since I was a DeVille, but it seemed like something Maverick wanted to handle on his own.

"The holidays are the worst, don't you think?" His misery was palpable, and his tone was condescending. Even with a drink in his hand and a suit, he still didn't look like he belonged there. His dark hair was combed back and he carried himself like an aristocrat, but I could have picked him out of the crowd in a heartbeat.

"Not if you have someone to spend them with."

"The one person I want to spend this holiday with isn't here..." With one hand resting in the pocket of his slacks, he brought the glass of champagne to his lips and took a drink. He admired the enormous tree for a moment before his gaze turned back to me.

"You have two other people you should want to spend the holidays with..." My father was probably happy to be reunited with my mother, but I knew he would miss spending the holidays with me. I could never compete with his love for my mother, but I always felt just as important. The desires that drove this man were perplexing.

"They don't want to spend the holidays with me, so it doesn't matter."

"It does matter," I corrected. "Because they do want to spend the holidays with you...if you just dropped this attitude and became a father again." Maybe I should be scared that he'd caught me off guard. Maybe I should be scared that he was there at all. But we were surrounded by a crowd full of people. The only way he would be able to kill me was by pulling out a gun and shooting me right on the spot. Everyone would know he was a murderer, and he wouldn't be able to show his face in public ever again. Caspian was too smart for that, so he was there for a different reason. "If you came here to intimidate me, it won't work. I'm not afraid of you."

"You aren't?" he asked almost comically. "Then you're very stupid or...just stupid. I'm a very dangerous man. Maverick obviously hasn't told you about the things I've done—"

"I don't find you dangerous. You want to know why?" I grabbed a glass of champagne from a passing waiter. "Because a dangerous man doesn't convince me to go back to my husband. He doesn't play cupid for his son. He doesn't give any kind of warning before he pulls the trigger. You care about your son. You aren't very good at expressing that and you're clearly embarrassed by it for some reason, but it's obvious that you do."

His expression fell into a cold simmer.

"So, no, I'm not afraid of you. I'm afraid that you're going to take too long to make things right with Maverick and he'll never forgive you. That's what I'm worried about. If you don't want to spend this Christmas alone or every Christmas afterward, then drop this disdain. Let it go, Caspian. There's still time to make things right... Don't piss away your last chance."

"So, children anytime soon?" An older gentleman holding a cocktail asked Maverick the question. With his wife beside them, they were another pair of aristocrats I hadn't met. No matter how many parties I attended, there always seemed to be someone new to meet.

I joined their conversation as Maverick absorbed the question and considered his response. "I think we want to enjoy each other a little longer. We're still newlyweds...even though we've been married almost a year."

"Isn't that sweet?" his wife said. "Enjoy the phase as long as you want."

My hand gently touched Maverick's arm, and I politely excused us both. "Let me borrow my husband for just a moment." I guided him away so we could speak in private in the center of the crowded room.

"Thank you for rescuing me. I'm not even sure who those people are."

"You invited them."

He shrugged. "I'm terrible with names. Even more terrible with faces."

"Well, I hope you never forget mine."

"Never." His arm moved around my waist, his fingertips gripping the fabric of my dress as he pulled me closer. His handsome face was close to mine, affection bright in his eyes. He probably wished everyone in that room would disappear so we could have a moment to ourselves.

I almost forgot the reason I wanted to talk to him. "Your father is here..."

His fingers slackened on the back of my dress as his eyes changed. They were affectionate just a second ago, but now they were steaming with hostility. He didn't raise his gaze to scan the crowd in search of his archnemesis. "You're certain?"

"We had a pretty hefty conversation...so, yes."

He dropped his hand from my waist altogether. "Did he hurt you?"

"No."

"What did he want?"

"Honestly, I'm not sure." My eyes scanned the people around us, and I did my best to seem calm, like Maverick and I were having a lighthearted conversation instead of an extremely tense one. "I told him I wasn't afraid of him. He didn't appreciate that very much."

"You should be afraid of him."

"Why would I when you're here?"

His eyes stayed locked on mine for several heartbeats, his face a closed curtain. His eyes remained indecipherable as he processed the situation and the appropriate response. A million thoughts sped through his mind, all traveling at the speed of light. "What's his game?" He pulled his eyes away from my face and looked around the room as he searched for Caspian in a sea of faces.

"No idea. But I don't think he's as threatening as he pretends to be. If he were, he wouldn't have persuaded me to come back to you. He would have broken my neck at the rehab center. He wouldn't be coming to a holiday party."

"You shouldn't assume."

"I don't like your father, but I think he misses his family...and doesn't know how to fix things."

He shook his head. "I took a bullet for him, and it meant nothing to him."

"Maybe he's had a change of heart."

"That man doesn't have a heart to change in the first place. Stay by my side for the rest of the night. I don't want to take any chances." His eyes kept scanning, and he didn't bother to pretend everything was okay for everyone else in the crowd.

Caspian was a despicable man with a maniacal sense of reality. After losing his wife, he forgot what love felt like. He forgot what his kids meant to him. I definitely didn't like him, but I wasn't completely convinced of his evilness. I believed there was a chance, however small, that Caspian would realize the error of his ways...and pull his head out of his ass.

14

MAVERICK

My father crashed my holiday party and conversed with everyone like he belonged there. A trick was up his sleeve because I could never get him to attend any of my functions when we were still allies. He was only doing this to taunt me, to remind me that my wife was still at the top of his kill list.

Now I really wanted to kill him.

My finger had never been able to squeeze the trigger, but when my wife's life was on the line, my finger wasn't so hesitant.

Keeping up conversations with my guests was practically impossible because my mind was elsewhere. Arwen stayed at my side like I asked her to and did a better job pretending everything was perfectly fine. It was her mistake not to take my father seriously, but I wouldn't let her pay the price for her stupidity.

I finally spotted him several feet away, holding a glass of champagne while engaged in conversation with one of my guests. He sipped his drink then laughed at whatever comment was just said, fitting right in with the festivities. I turned my lips to her ear. "Stay here." My arms slid from around her waist, and I walked across the room as I approached my father, the notorious asshole.

"You have a lovely holiday as well," my father said as he finished his conversation. He hardly looked at me but seemed to understand I was there. He took another drink of his champagne then faced me. "I noticed you haven't had a drink all night. Expecting?"

After my horrific night on the town, I still hadn't regained my appetite for booze. The scotch had burned a hole in my liver, and the idea of alcohol still didn't seem appealing to me. I was a man with booze in my system nearly all the time, but I'd realized I'd hit my limit. Now it was time to take a step back and let my body cleanse itself. "It's pathetic to stir up trouble at a Christmas party. I thought you had more honor than that."

"All is fair in love and war, right?" He smiled before he took another drink from his glass. With one hand in his pocket while a perfectly tailored suit hugged his muscular frame, he behaved like this was a perfectly normal conversation.

"For cowards, yes."

His gentle smile disappeared, and he turned his expression on me. "You're the coward, Maverick. Your wife betrayed our family, and you allowed it to happen."

"I didn't allow it. I had no idea what her ambition was. If I had known, I probably wouldn't have stopped her, but that's beside the point. I didn't know."

"You know now, but you choose to do nothing."

"Because I stand by my wife's side. She did the right thing, and you know it. That's what Mom would have wanted, it's what Lily wanted, and it's what I wanted. The three of us are still a family. You're the one who's dead—not Mom."

He appeared crestfallen, punctured by what I'd said like a knife had been stabbed into his lung. He lowered his glass and stared at me with unblinking eyes, as if he were repeating my words in his mind over and over again. Speechless, he continued to stand there like he didn't know what else to do.

It was the first time my words had wounded him. It was the first time I'd had any kind of impact on this heartless man. The fog around his gaze had finally dissipated, and he listened to something that flew out of my mouth. My speech came from the heart, but I didn't expect it to have any kind of emotional impact whatsoever.

But it seemed to mean something to him...finally.

ONCE THE PARTY was over and the guests were cleared out of the house, Arwen and I headed upstairs to bed. It was nearly three in the morning, and she'd had too much champagne because she could barely walk.

She gripped the banister to steady herself as she carried herself up the stairs. When she lost her balance, she held on tighter and righted herself. Then a loud laugh escaped her lips, like she found the whole scene comical. "I thought I tripped, but then I realized I didn't trip...but then I did trip."

I turned around and came back to her. "Too much champagne tonight?"

"Looks like I'm a drunk mess just like you." She laughed again.

I scooped her into my arms then cradled her against my chest. Even up three flights of stairs, she was like carrying a pile of feathers. I made my way to the second landing then proceeded to the third.

Her arms locked around my neck, and she rested her cheek against my chest. "Big, strong man..."

Even though my night had been overshadowed by the tense

conversation with my father, an involuntary chuckle escaped my lips. "You're just small."

"I'm not that small."

We reached the third landing, and I carried her into the bedroom.

"I'm so drunk right now, but I still want sex. Good sex."

I set her on the bed then peeled off my jacket. "Sounds good to me."

"You don't mind taking advantage of your wife?" She rose to her feet then unzipped the back of her dress. It fell to the floor and revealed her naked form and her sheer thong. She peeled that down her legs and didn't bother taking off her heels. She got back into bed.

"No." I turned around and removed my tie and collared shirt. My foul mood couldn't chase away the arousal I felt in that moment. My drunk wife was asking for sex, and I was happy to deliver. I took off my slacks and shoes then peeled off my boxers.

When I turned around, she was asleep.

Flat on her back with her hair a mess across the pillows, she'd fallen into a deep sleep almost instantly. Her lips were parted, and she gave a quiet snore because she was so tired.

I approached the bed and swallowed my disappointment. It would be easy for me to wake her up, but disturbing her seemed innately wrong. Even when she was a mess on the bed, she was still angelically beautiful. I grabbed each ankle and got her sparkly heels off before I pulled down the covers and tucked her in.

I took care of her just the way she took care of me.

That night, I'd been so embarrassed by my stupid behavior. I never allowed myself to be weak, to be in a position when I couldn't take care of myself. I could barely walk, but my wife was by my side the entire time.

Now I did the same for her.

Marriage wasn't just about fidelity and honesty. It was about being there for each other equally... I was starting to learn that.

I turned off the lights and got into bed beside her.

She wasn't usually a snorer, but she started to snore like a water buffalo.

I lay in bed with my arm propped under my head as I stared at the ceiling. The party had been a success, and I'd found more partnerships than I'd expected to gain. But seeing my father there had thrown off my entire mood. He was the black cloud in my sky, the tick of a bomb about to explode. He was a nuisance that wouldn't go away, a person determined to ruin the brighter moments of my life. Maybe all of that was about to change.

Or maybe it was about to get worse.

15

ARWEN

The second I opened my eyes, I knew I was hungover. I wanted to pull the sheets over my head and ignore the sunlight poking through the curtains. The only reason I wanted to wake up was to pop a couple of pills and swallow them with a glass of water.

How much champagne did I drink last night?

When a knock sounded on the door, Maverick opened it, exchanged brief words with Abigail, and then returned to the bed. "Get up."

"No..."

"You have to face the day sometime."

"No, I don't."

"Abigail brought breakfast, including your favorite jam."

My eyes opened. "Yeah?"

"Yeah." The weight of the bed tray dipped into the mattress beside me. "Now, get up and eat."

I finally pulled the sheets down and cringed at the sunlight. "Why are all the blinds open...?"

"Because it's noon."

"You want me to go blind? When you were too drunk to function, I kept this place as dark as a planetarium."

He stayed on the bed for a second as if he wanted to resist my request, but then he caved and walked to all the curtains and closed them.

"Much better." I picked up a piece of toast and smeared jam across the bread.

He sat up in bed beside me, dressed in sweatpants without a shirt. His hair was styled like he'd already taken a shower and started his day. A cup of coffee was on the nightstand beside him, so he sipped it as he watched me eat. "Headache?"

"Three."

"Three headaches?" he asked in bewilderment.

"Yes...it feels like three headaches."

He grabbed the bottle off his nightstand and dropped a few pills into his hand. He placed them on the bed tray. "That should get you moving."

I swallowed them dry then kept eating. There were also scrambled eggs and a couple of pancakes, but I only took a few bites because I wasn't that hungry. I focused on the freshly baked toast and the jam that came from Abigail's secret recipe. "Did you have a good time last night?"

He held the mug between his hands on his lap. "As good of a time as I could have."

"I liked it, and not just because I didn't have to sing."

"And my father didn't disgruntle you at all?" He brought his mug to his lips and took another drink.

"No. Did he disgruntle you?" I'd kept drinking throughout the night and never asked if Maverick had confronted his father. Caspian may be a dangerous man, but my instinct told me not to be afraid of him. He may be a terrible father, but he wouldn't kill his son's wife...even if he wanted to. He had the perfect opportunity in that bar, but he didn't take it. He put his son first...because he loved him.

"We said a few things...then he walked away."

"And what was said?"

He stared into his coffee mug for a while, the liquid matching the color of his eyes. He brought it to his lips and took a long drink before he answered. "I told him my mother wasn't dead. He's the one's who's dead."

I ignored my toast because his words were more powerful than my appetite. I dropped the jam-smeared bread back on the tray and gave him my full attention. "What did he say to that?"

"Nothing. He walked off."

It was a brilliant thing for Maverick to say, a shockingly accurate description of his father. His mother was gone, but her spirit kept Maverick alive. She continued to give him hope and inspiration. His father was the one who changed so much he was hardly recognizable. "I wonder how he felt about that."

He shrugged. "He would never tell me."

I picked up the tray and moved it aside so I could sit directly beside Maverick. My pounding headache would have to be ignored so this conversation could continue. There was nothing that haunted him more than his complicated relationship with his father. "I think your father is sad, lonely, and lost...and he doesn't know what to do about it. Killing Ramon didn't make him feel better, and he knows killing Ramon's wife wouldn't have made a difference either. But he needs something to focus on because he has nothing left. He misses you and Lily, but he doesn't know how to fix that relationship. He doesn't know where to start."

"You give him too much credit."

"No. I'm not saying he's a good man. I'm just saying he's very mentally ill and doesn't know how to fix it."

Maverick kept looking into his mug.

"I know you don't want to, and you shouldn't even have to, but I think you should reach out to him...give him an olive branch."

"I hope that's a joke. You know how many olive branches I've extended?"

"I know... But try again."

He shook his head. "I need to kill him. I'll always look over my shoulder until I know he's gone."

"There's another option..."

"I don't think there is, Arwen." He set his mug on the night-stand. "I've tried fixing my relationship with my father many times. I've proven my loyalty a million times over. But he doesn't care about those instances. He only cares about my betrayals."

It was wrong for me to inject my opinion into something so complicated. Maverick had been hurt by this abusive relationship so many times that his emotions were a wide spectrum of pain. I couldn't understand everything he'd been through because this had been going on long before we met. "I understand why you're angry at him. I understand why you even hate him. But I think he was a man deeply in love who lost his wife. His mind snapped, and it was easier to be hateful than feel all the pain. When he looks at you and Lily, he probably sees your mother...and that's hard for him."

"Even if that's true, that's supposed to be okay?"

"No. Not at all. I'm just explaining his behavior. Now that he's had enough time to cope, to kill Ramon, he's probably at a dead end. His survival strategies don't work anymore, and now he's forced to face reality. He could have killed me, but he didn't. Instead, he guided me back to you. That speaks volumes."

He was quiet.

"And when I spoke to him at the rehab center, I think that was a wake-up call for him too. He witnessed me working to repair your relationship, not tear it apart, and I risked my safety to do it. He's never said it, but I can tell he respects me for my actions."

Maverick had nothing to say.

"I think you should try one more time, Maverick."

"If he can crash my Christmas party, he can make a phone call. He can stop by the house for a conversation. You're acting like he needs help facilitating this, but that's ridiculous. He can do anything he wants—if he wants to do it."

"Maybe he has too much pride—"

"Then he needs to suck it up." The temperature of the room rose slightly, matching the palpable rage exuding from his core. The conversation was over the second he snapped. "He's done enough damage. It's time he starts fixing it."

"I just think—"

"This is over." He shut down the conversation with his tone, the vein in his forehead starting to protrude underneath the skin. He kept his eyes straight ahead, rage and indifference mixed together within his gaze. His gentle breaths turned to deep inhales of air.

Slowly, he calmed himself once more, letting the silence absorb the hostility that filled the room just seconds ago.

Since he wasn't in the mood, I didn't press further. "Do you have plans tomorrow?"

He grabbed the coffee mug off the nightstand. "No."

"You don't spend the holidays with Lily?"

"She wants to stay in the rehab facility. She has a few friends coming."

Tomorrow was Christmas Day. It was the first holiday I would celebrate without my father. We used to exchange gifts on Christmas Eve and then have dinner on Christmas Day. It would be impossible to really cherish the holiday without him. "So, it's just the two of us?"

He nodded. "Just the two of us."

"That sounds nice..." It was my first Christmas as a married woman. There wouldn't be a big feast with family members gathered around, but at least we weren't alone. We always had each other...until we started a family. "My father and I used to exchange gifts on Christmas Eve while we ate pie."

"My family used to do the same too. Want to exchange gifts tonight?" Now that the conversation about his father had been shut down, his mood picked up slightly.

The offer surprised me. "You got me something?" I picked out a nice collared shirt that would look perfect against his olive complexion and dark hair. It wasn't of designer quality, but since he was so fit, it would probably look great on him anyway. But I hadn't expected him to do the same for me.

He turned his head in my direction, locking his gaze on mine for the first time. "Of course I did."

MAVERICK SHOWERED THEN WENT across the hall to his office to finish up a couple of things before we would share a bottle of wine and exchange gifts under the Christmas tree. We'd spent the afternoon in bed, making love, talking, and eating. That was already magical. And now it was about to get better.

But Caspian kept crossing my mind.

Caspian said one thing but did the exact opposite. He threatened to kill me, but he let me go without a scratch, and he showed up to the Christmas party without causing a scene. He seemed to be in such a deep pit that he couldn't get out of it...couldn't apologize and make things right with this son.

That's what I believed, at least.

While Maverick was distracted, I wanted to take my car and drive to Caspian's place to make things right.

But my husband would never forgive me. I promised I wouldn't sneak off like that ever again, and I had to keep that promise. How could I expect him to keep his word if I never kept mine?

That meant I could only make a phone call.

That wasn't breaking the rules.

Getting Caspian's number was easy because Maverick left his phone in the bedroom. I managed to pull up old conversations and write down the phone number. Then I went to my old room and locked the door behind me. My clothes still hung in the closet, and my accessories were on the counter. I'd never officially moved in with him, but I suspected that would happen soon.

I sat on the edge of the bed and made the call.

Ring.

Ring.

Ring.

It was Christmas Eve, so maybe he wouldn't pick up. I doubted he had plans for the evening. He didn't seem like a man with many friends—only enemies.

He finally answered. "This better be important." His voice came out as an annoyed growl. He didn't even know who I was or what I wanted, and his immediate impulse was to be an asshole.

"It is." I let the sound of my voice do all the talking. He didn't know me very well, but he would guess my identity quickly.

When he was quiet for a couple of seconds, it was obvious he'd figured it out. "Nice party last night. I had a great time."

"It didn't seem like it."

"Anytime there's a drink in my hand, I'm in a decent mood."

"Then I wish you were drunk all the time," I countered. "Perhaps you would be a good father...and a decent father-in-law."

He chuckled even though there was nothing funny about this. "I doubt it. And I underestimated you. When I married you off to my son, I assumed you were a dumb pretty girl. I guess I was wrong."

"Very wrong." Caspian had treated me like a shadow since the day he met me. He never introduced himself and barely said a few words...even though I would be the mother of his grand-children.

"I'm not much of a chatter, so if there's something you want to say, get on with it."

"An asshole...as always."

"Now you know where Maverick gets it from."

"Your son is not an asshole," I said firmly. "He's one of the greatest men I've ever known. And he gets that from his mother—not you."

When Caspian didn't laugh off my comment, I knew it had pierced his invincible armor. "What do you want?"

"I want you to bury the hatchet and make things right with Maverick. It's what I've always wanted—and I know you want the same thing. You came to that Christmas party without any agenda. If you weren't there to cause trouble, then what were you doing?"

"Maybe I just wanted a drink."

"You can get a drink anywhere, Caspian."

"Then maybe I was there to kill you."

"It didn't seem like it. What were you planning to do? Stab me in the middle of a crowded room?"

"I've done it before."

I was certain he had. "But that wasn't why you were there, and we both know it."

Silence.

"Come over tomorrow. Spend Christmas with your son."

More silence.

"Caspian?"

"No."

"So, you'd rather spend Christmas alone?"

Silence.

"Caspian," I pressed. "Apologize to your son and put this behind you. He will forgive you. I know you don't want it to be like this, but you don't know how to fix it. Apologizing to Maverick is a good start."

"I'm not apologizing to him."

This man was more stubborn than his own son. "Why?"

He returned to his favorite response—silence.

"Caspian, if you wait too long, you'll lose your chance altogether. As each day passes, Maverick becomes more bitter. Wait too long, and he'll be indifferent to you. He won't need an apology because he won't care about your relationship anymore."

Nothing.

"Maybe your behavior feels justified because you lost your wife. But remember that Maverick and Lily lost their mother. They're hurting too. It's not just you. I know you were lost in your despair and things got out of hand. You didn't even realize how bad things were until recently. But if you just apologize, you can both move on from this—"

"I'm not apologizing, Arwen. Maybe my kids deserve an apology, but I'm not giving it to them. I've been an asshole for a long time, and a few simple words aren't going to make a difference."

"You'd be surprised..."

"Maverick doesn't want me in his life, and that's fine."

"That's not true...he does want you in his life. But he wants his father, not this dark tyrant that threatens to kill everyone all the time."

He sighed into the phone.

"Why won't you just apologize? I know you don't want to kill me. I know you don't want things to be this bad with Maverick. I understand you have a lot of pride, but pride is a flaw in a man, not a quality."

He was quiet for a long time, like he would prefer silence as his response. But then he spoke, surprising me. "When Maverick faced Kamikaze for Russian roulette, I placed one of my guys in the room. His job was to make sure the bullet was in the right chamber and to make sure Maverick went first."

All the muscles in my body tensed as my lungs stopped working. That afternoon had been one of the worst days of my life. I'd thought I could lose my husband at any moment. Every time their fingers squeezed the trigger, I was both relieved and terrified. Now that I knew Caspian been pulling the strings behind the scenes, my heart tightened all over again. "Tell him that."

"No."

"He should hear it from you, not me."

"No."

I couldn't comprehend this kind of stubbornness. "Are you embarrassed?"

Silence.

"So, you'll save your son's life, you'll convince his wife to return to him, but you won't apologize?"

After a long pause, he responded. "Enjoy your Christmas, Arwen." Then he hung up.

I set the phone on the bed beside me and crossed my arms over my chest. I couldn't believe the conversation I'd just had. While I gained more information, I was no closer to getting these two men back together. Caspian would never apologize to his son. The only option I had was getting Maverick to go to him...but that seemed just as impossible.

WE SAT on the rug in front of the Christmas tree, presents tucked under the branches. It was a cold night, the kind where the frozen air pressed frost against the windows. A fire burned in the large hearth, and we shared a bottle of wine, skipping the glasses and going straight for the bottle.

Maverick leaned against the armchair and stared at me, dressed in his sweatpants with a black t-shirt. Every time he took a drink of wine, he licked his lips, and he made it look so sexy. His hair was styled, and his powerful chest stretched his t-shirt. The Christmas party was no longer on his mind, and he was calm and carefree. He must have stopped thinking about his father.

"Open mine first." I grabbed the medium-sized box and handed it to him. Wrapped in white paper with holly leaves on the front, it was a present I'd wrapped myself. Abigail would have done it for me, but it seemed a lot more special if I did it myself.

He took the box and examined it, as if he was trying to guess what it was before he ripped into it. "Hmm...lingerie?"

I rolled my eyes. "No."

"Are you lying?"

"Why would I get you lingerie for Christmas? You're beautiful, but I don't think it'd look good on you."

"But it would look perfect on you." He shook the box, and the sound of the material inside made it obvious it was a piece of clothing. "Ooh...that's a good sign."

"Open it."

After he gave me that handsome smile, he slid his thumb under the wrapping and ripped through the tape. He pulled it apart until he got to the white box underneath. After ripping through more tape, he opened the lid and revealed the wine-colored collared shirt.

"I know it's not fancy like the stuff you normally wear..."

He held up the shirt and examined the front, the sleeves stretching down. "I love it." He set it down again and popped open all the buttons so the shirt would come loose. He pushed his arms through the sleeves and got it on before he buttoned the front once more. "Fits perfectly."

It did look good on him, just as nice as his designer clothes. Sometimes, I used to picture what my life would be like, how I would spend the holidays with my husband. I imagined buying him presents and watching him open them under the tree. Fantasy was never as good as reality...but this was. It felt right. It didn't feel like this was an arranged marriage neither one of us wanted. Now it felt like we were two people deeply in love... spending Christmas together. "It looks nice on you."

"Thank you." He came to my side and sat beside me against the couch. One arm moved over my shoulders, and he leaned in to kiss me, his lips tasting like the wine we'd been drinking. His hand supported the back of my head as his mouth moved with mine, giving me more than just a simple kiss.

The flames were warm against our skin even from this distance, and the smell of pine needles entered my nose and made it feel like Christmas. But neither of those were as magical as the kiss we just shared. It felt like a fairy tale.

He pulled away and allowed his fingers to explore my hair, his eyes full of affection and something deeper. "Now open yours."

I grabbed the small box and set it in my lap. "I already know what it is."

"Do you?" he asked, his smile widening.

"Lingerie, obviously."

He chuckled. "Open it and find out."

I ripped through the wrapping and opened the box underneath. Inside was a black picture frame. Inside was a picture of us...on our wedding day. The photographer got a picture of us dancing together, his head bent down to kiss me. I remembered the moment perfectly. All the guests clanked their spoons against their glasses and enticed us to kiss, so we did. In that moment, I'd felt the jolt of attraction, the undeniable chemistry that started to burn our first day as husband and wife. I remembered that kiss so well, I could actually still feel his lips against mine. My eyes couldn't pull away from the picture because I was so entranced by the memory. "I love it…"

"I love it too."

I stared at it a bit longer before I turned my gaze back to him, not even aware of the tears that were in my eyes. "So sweet…"

"I guess I can be sweet…for you." His fingers brushed the hair away from my face so he could get a better look at me. With a new expression he hadn't shown in the past, he watched me for a long time, a mixture of a million emotions deep in his gaze.

If I hadn't known it before, I certainly knew it now… I loved this man.

He leaned his forehead against mine then closed his eyes, embracing me in front of the Christmas tree and the fireplace. Our gifts were quickly forgotten as we became wrapped up in each other, cherishing the silence as well as our gentle breathing. We were tender and loving, and it seemed like I wasn't the only one that felt this way…like I wasn't the only one deeply in love. Maverick had been a different man when he became my husband, and he'd slowly morphed into someone I couldn't live without. He was strong, brutish, and stubborn, but he was also loving, devoted, and affectionate. His rough edges became soft like pillows, and all the hostility he possessed turned into something kinder.

His fingers massaged my hair, gently playing with it as he held me close. "I love you."

My eyes were closed, but I pictured the way his lips moved as he said those words. The sound of his voice was so beautiful, just like the sound of the crackling flames in the fireplace. His tone was deep and masculine but also sincere, and the words were the sexiest thing I'd ever heard him say. It made me warm from my fingertips to my toes.

When I opened my eyes, I felt the tears slip down my cheeks. "I love you too..."

He pulled away so he could look at me, so his thumbs could catch my tears. "I'm sorry that I wasn't the best husband when we first got married. But I'll be the husband you want every day for the rest of my life."

"You are the best husband... I wouldn't change anything about you. You were there for me when I lost my father. You were there for me when I needed to be saved. You were there for me when I needed a friend. I don't love the way we got here, but I wouldn't change any of it for anything. I would do it all again in a heartbeat."

He brought our faces close together again. "I never wanted a wife. But now I can't imagine being with any woman besides you. I want you every day for the rest of my life. I want to be buried beside you until the sun burns out. I want to have children with you...grow old with you."

My hands cupped his face as more tears spilled down my cheeks. "Me too..."

THE SOUND of the fire in the hearth was unnoticeable because our heavy breathing drowned it out. We'd spend the early part of the day screwing, but now we moved together like that never happened. With my ankles locked together at the top of his ass, I rocked with him as he drove deep inside me.

Over and over.

My fingers cherished the feeling of his powerful back, starting at his shoulders and making their way down the flanks of muscle that hugged his spine. When he hit me in just the right place, my nails came out like claws, and I carved into his back, leaving scratches that would last for days.

He was always so beautiful when he was sexy and fatigued. His body always performed to its full potential to please me, the muscles working hard to lift his body and then slide it back down so he could ram his cock deep inside me.

I loved making love to my husband. "Maverick…" I no longer felt the rush of lust that used to swell inside my veins. Now, I felt the deep passion that stemmed from love, that grew from a lifelong commitment neither one of us would break. I wanted this man for the rest of my life. I'd never wanted a poor replacement, a substitute that could never compare.

My fingers scratched at his ass before they moved into his hair once more. I ground my hips and rocked with his movements, so close to a climax I could already feel it. My toes curled preemptively, and my limbs clenched as my body constricted around him.

He must have felt me tighten around him because he started to pound me into hard, driving me into an orgasm that brought tears to my eyes. His powerful ass worked hard to give it to me good, to give me every inch so deeply.

My arms latched on to his body, and I gripped him firmly as I rode the high, my blood burning because it felt so good. When I came with other lovers, the tears never sprang to my eyes because the sex had never been so good. Only one man could make me cry—and that was my husband.

He watched my expression change as it showed all my feelings, as my mouth flew open with a moan and my eyes watered with emotion. My cheeks flushed bright red, and I bit my bottom lip so I wouldn't scream right in his face. He loved the performance I gave. It was obvious in the way his expression became so focused, the way his eyes didn't blink because he didn't want to miss a single second.

My face moved into his neck as I finished. The euphoria became overwhelming, so powerful that I needed to shield my look just so I could tolerate it. I gripped my husband like he was a life vest and held on for dear life.

It felt amazing to the very last second. Once the high passed, my body released and the tears stopped.

Oh god, that felt so good.

Maverick continued to rock into me, his cock hardening just a little more as he prepared to finish.

I pulled my face away from the crook of his shoulder and met his look once again. My ring dragged along my chest as he moved, tapping against me with his thrusts. I watched him work to reach his climax, watched his glistening body move hard and fast to get to the end. His powerful arms pressed into the bed and kept his body up as he worked his hips. Deeper and deeper, he drove until he hit his threshold.

With a sexy moan, he came inside me.

I grabbed his ass and pulled him deeper, wanting every drop he could give. Sometimes his climaxes were better than mine just because I could feel his seed deep inside me. I moaned when I felt him fill me, felt my husband give himself to me.

The memory of the other women was long forgotten because it didn't seem important anymore. It didn't seem to matter at all—to either of us.

When he finished, he kissed me softly on the mouth, giving me a kiss that was slow but still passionate. His dick softened inside me, but he still made me full anyway, made me feel like the most desirable woman in the world.

The woman he loved.

He gently pulled out of me then rolled onto his back, his body softening now that he could relax. He didn't have to excuse himself to the bathroom to wash off like he used to. Now we could just lie together when we were finished, tangled up in each other's arms in mutual satisfaction.

He lay on his side and looked at me, his chest rising and falling more slowly now that his body had caught up on rest. A shadow was along his jawline, and his coffee-colored eyes were filled with a brighter hue. His new shirt lay on the ground, and my picture frame was on his nightstand. Well, my nightstand now.

My hand went to his chest and touched the ring that hung on the chain. The diamond was as bold and brilliant as ever, a reminder of the commitment I'd made to him. I wanted to wear it because I missed it. I also wanted to wear it because I was ready to be everything we promised. I was ready to be his dutiful wife, the woman who would take care of him and put up with his bullshit for all eternity.

He kept his eyes on me.

My hands moved to the back of his neck so I could unclasp the chain.

He grabbed both of my wrists then brought them to his lips for a kiss. "I'll give it to you some other time."

"Why can't I have it now?"

He kissed my hands again. "Because I'm not ready to give it to you yet."

16

MAVERICK

CHRISTMAS MORNING WAS JUST A CONTINUATION OF CHRISTMAS Eve.

Perfect.

Abigail left breakfast in front of the door so we could take it whenever we wanted it. We spent the morning lying in bed in front of the fire, watching Christmas movies, and being snuggled up together under the sheets.

Lots of lovemaking happened in between.

I'd never fucked the same woman so much in my life. And I'd never made love to someone before. It didn't matter how slow and mediocre the pace seemed from the outside. It felt so good in the moment, even when we were barely moving because we spent most of our energy kissing.

It felt good to be in love.

My wife was amazing. I wouldn't change a thing about her. I hated my father so much, but now I was grateful he made me agree to this arrangement. If I hadn't...this never would have happened. I would have been a lonely bachelor with no sense of belonging. It would have been unfulfilling...and depressing.

She snuggled into my side and kissed my shoulder. "When did you know?"

She could have been asking a million different things, but I knew exactly what was on her mind. "I've always known."

"Always?" she asked incredulously. "That seems unlikely."

"I did... I always knew." I'd played Russian roulette with a psychopath to buy her freedom. I wouldn't have done that for just anyone. Maybe my sister and maybe Kent, but that was it. I wouldn't have chased away her admirers unless I felt like I owned her in some way. I wouldn't have been scarred by the sight of Brandon in her apartment if I didn't love her. "I don't know when it happened exactly. It was so slow and unnoticeable at first. I always knew it was there but pretended I didn't. When you told me how you felt, I couldn't lie anymore. It forced me to confront my feelings, but I was too much of a coward to do it. Having you back has made me so happy that I couldn't contain it anymore. It just slipped out."

"Well, I'm glad that it slipped out. I always thought you felt the same way. When you took on Kamikaze, I didn't believe you did that out of obligation. It seemed like it was more meaningful than that."

I would have given my life for her because I wanted to. "It was."

She rubbed her hand across my chest then pressed another kiss to my shoulder. "When Kamikaze was gone, you didn't ask me to leave. We could have gotten a divorce, but you never asked for one."

"Because I didn't want to be divorced. I didn't want to admit that I loved you...so I just didn't think about it. But now it's all I can think about."

Her fingers continued to caress my body, to feel the hardness of my muscles and the softness of my skin. "I loved you a long time ago...even when I still hated you."

"You hated me and loved me at the same time?"

"Yes..."

I smiled slightly. "I'm hard to love, so I believe that."

"You aren't hard to love anymore. You make loving so easy." She leaned into me and pressed a kiss to the corner of my mouth. When she was finished, she rested her forehead against my chin and stayed there for a while. The happiness was suddenly sucked out of the room as if by a vacuum, and a foreboding feeling replaced it. She didn't say a single word, but her energy was distinct. We were perfect just a second ago, so what had changed so drastically?

I pulled away so I could look directly into her gaze, see her expression head on. "What is it?"

A forced smile stretched her mouth. "You know me so well, don't you?"

"You're my wife." Now I was used to saying that phrase, letting it roll off my tongue so easily. "I know you pretty damn well."

"Well...hear me out, alright?"

My eyes narrowed.

She leaned against the wooden headboard and stared at me. "I talked to your father yesterday..."

It took less than a few seconds for the calmness in my blood to evaporate like boiling water. My serenity was washed away and replaced by revulsion. A sense of betrayal swept through me. She told me she would never pull a stunt like that ever again, but she did it anyway. "He could have killed you—"

"I talked to him over the phone," she said quickly. "I never left the house."

Relief started in my shoulders then slowly migrated everywhere else. I was still annoyed she'd talked to him at all, but at least the terms were better. I stared at the flames for a few minutes to calm down before I shifted my gaze back to her. "And?"

"And...I think you should talk to him."

"That's a joke, right?" The asshole crashed my Christmas party and tossed around a couple of threats. I wasn't going to call him just so I could hear more—especially on Christmas.

"I understand why you have no motivation to reach out to him. He's been extremely difficult and doesn't deserve your patience. But I think you should try anyway."

"And say what, exactly? What's the point of this conversation?" I'd tried to be there for my father over the last two years, but he continually disappointed me. That man was so far gone that he would never come back.

"Bury the hatchet."

I raised an eyebrow. "Let me get this straight. He's the one who's been a fucking pain in the ass, but I'm the one who's supposed to fix everything? He has my number, so if he wanted to apologize, he could do it at any moment. The ball has been in his court for a long time. I've been a good son—but he hasn't been a good father."

"I know...you shouldn't have to make any effort. But I think you should."

"No." I turned my gaze away.

"Maverick..."

"I took a bullet for that man. I married a stranger for that man.

I've done everything for that man. If he wants to make things right with me, he needs to do it. He owes me a big fucking apology."

"I know he does, but he's stubborn."

"What a coincidence," I said sarcastically. "So am I."

Her hand moved to my arm, and she rubbed it gently. "I don't know why this is hard for him, but it obviously is. He's not good at expressing himself or being vulnerable."

"Neither am I... I am his son."

"You're definitely better than he is."

"That's debatable."

"Please talk to him."

"Why is this so important to you?" I turned back to her.

"Because he's your father, Maverick. I know you still love him... and I know he loves you."

My father hadn't said those words to me since I was a child. I found it unlikely that he loved anyone. Now I wasn't even sure if he loved my mother since he was willing to rape and kill two innocent women. She never would have wanted that. "He threatened to kill my wife..."

"But he never did."

"And that makes it okay?" I asked incredulously. "The guy is a psychopath, and you know it."

"I think he's just a broken man who needs help...but is too stubborn to ask for it."

"What do you expect me to do? Go over there and apologize to him?"

"No."

"Demand him to apologize to me?"

She sighed. "No."

"Then what am I supposed to do?"

She squeezed my arm. "Forgive him."

The request was so ridiculous, I wasn't sure if I'd heard her correctly. "How can you forgive someone when they don't apologize?"

"You can...as long as you love them."

Love certainly wasn't an emotion I felt toward my father. He'd made me so angry for the last few years. He'd disappointed me, hurt me.

"Just talk to him, Maverick. It's Christmas."

"So? He didn't remember my birthday."

"I'm sure he did, but it was too hard to acknowledge."

What kind of excuse was that?

"I know it's a lot to ask. I know you've been the victim of his behavior when you shouldn't be. I know he's the one who should be on his knees apologizing to you. But you need to be the bigger man and end this. If that's not enough reason for you, think about me."

Having no idea what she meant, I narrowed my eyes.

"If you bury the hatchet and forgive him, he'll have no reason to hurt me. Then you never have to worry about that."

Keeping her safe was always my top priority, and it was such a strange feeling to protect her from my own father. If he was willing to talk to me and drop this war, that alone would be worth it. Maybe he and I would never be close again. Maybe there was too much to forgive.

"Talk to him."

"It's Christmas."

"That's exactly why you should talk to him."

THE FRONT ENTRANCE was deserted because of the holiday. I pulled up to the house without being screened or being patted down for weapons. There were a few lights shining through the windows, but the place still felt deserted. Once upon a time, it used to be lively and warm. My family had dinner parties in the winter and barbecues in the summer. Not it looked like an abandoned house.

I moved to the front door and rang the doorbell. My father had cameras everywhere, so he would know it was me long before he opened the door. My wife was at home alone on Christmas, but she sent me here because it was important to her. Now I stood on the doorstep in my jeans and jacket, battling the cold outside.

A moment later, he opened the door. With the same hostile dark eyes as mine, he stared me up and down as if he was sizing me up as an opponent, not cherishing the sight of his only son on his doorstep.

I almost turned around and walked off.

Stubborn as always, my father didn't invite me inside and waited for me to speak first.

"Thought we could talk."

One hand stayed on the door, and his wide shoulders blocked the entryway so I couldn't invite myself inside. He regarded me like a stranger rather than his own flesh and blood. "Your wife put you up to this?"

"You think I would have come over here by my own choice?"

A ghost of a smile entered his lips, a slight brightness burning in his eyes. "She knows how to make things happen...impressive." He dropped his hand from the doorknob and turned to walk inside the house—leaving the opening clear for me. His powerful shoulders were straight as he walked into the house, carrying himself like a proud soldier. He snatched a bottle of aged scotch off the counter and carried it to the large dining room where we used to celebrate the holidays. The mahogany wood was just as elegant as I remembered with the exception of one scratch I'd made as a child.

I sat down and ran my fingers over the crack, feeling the slight dip that had been caused by my knife. Memories of my childhood came flooding back to me, all the good times I'd had in this house. I'd been lucky to have a good mother and father to raise me. Losing that blessing made me feel sick to my stomach every time I thought about it.

My father filled my glass then slid it across the table toward me.

I didn't drink it.

He took a drink from his own glass as he watched me with killer eyes. When he returned the glass to the table, it was with a noticeable thud. The solid wood made a formidable echo when anything tapped against it. "You aren't going to drink?"

"I've cut back." I pushed the glass to the side, still slightly repulsed by the sight of alcohol. There was some booze lingering in my bloodstream because I was so damn drunk a couple weeks ago.

"It doesn't look like you've cut back. Seems like you quit cold turkey."

"Just taking a break."

My father had no problem drinking alone. Without an ounce of self-consciousness, he brought the glass to his lips and took another drink.

I couldn't believe I was there. I was sitting across from the man I despised, my eyes locked on his with a mixture of annoyance and disbelief. How would this conversation even start? Where should we begin? I refused to apologize and so did he, so what kind of compromise could we find? "Arwen pressured me to come here today." It was a bland start, but it was something.

"She's pushy."

"Yes...a bit." My eyes moved away, and I looked at the paintings that had been on the walls since my childhood. There was a watering can with daisies poking out of the top. There was another painting of red germaniums overflowing from a jar. My mother always loved flowers. Instead of hiring a gardener, she tended to the flowers herself. It was only fitting that the flower paintings surrounded her portrait on the wall.

He stared at the glass between his fingertips.

The silence stretched on, and the more time that passed, the less inclined I was to speak.

He was the same way.

"She thinks we can reconcile." My hands rested on the table, and I interlocked my fingers like I was having a meeting I didn't really care about. "What do you think about that?" I knew I wanted my father to apologize to me, to show some sign of emotion, to be the man I remembered. I wanted my father back, not this grizzled and bitter man. There was still a possibility of putting this behind us, but I couldn't do all the work. I shouldn't have to.

He tipped his glass toward himself and peered inside to look at the contents. Even though there was no ice inside, he shook the glass gently before he took a drink. His tanned skin looked like weathered leather from being outside so much. His eyes matched the drink in his hand, and his thin lips were constantly pulled back in a slight grimace. He was such a hateful person, losing all sense of love the moment my mother's heart stopped beating. "That's a pretty big hatchet to bury."

I'd come all the way here on Christmas, and he was still being difficult. Why was I surprised? "As much as I want to kill you, the rest of my body won't cooperate. My finger won't squeeze the trigger because it feels so wrong. You once called me a coward because of it...I disagree. The young boy inside me still remembers when you bought me my first fire truck and taught me how to play football. If I kill you now, then there's no possibility of this relationship getting better...and I don't want to end that possibility if I don't have to. You haven't been my father for a really long time, but the stupid boy inside me still believes you might come back...that a miracle might happen." I couldn't look him in the eye as I spoke because it was too humiliating. My masculinity was at stake when I poured my heart out like this, when I showed my vulnerability. The only person who saw me like this was my wife—and that was already difficult enough. "I don't know how I disappointed you as a son when I'm proud of who I am. I don't know how losing Mom could make you so indifferent to the two children you made with her. If she were alive now, she would be so disappointed in you. She's not here anymore, so it's your job to love her children—and you failed miserably. You should apologize to Lily and me and hope we have the compassion to forgive you."

His hand released his glass, and his elbows rested on the table. He watched me quietly, his eyes still and his breathing almost unnoticeable. He was difficult to read because his face lacked any expression. We were the same in that regard. I was almost impossible to read...as my wife pointed out.

He hadn't threatened to kill me yet, so that was a good sign. I didn't expect him to break down in tears and admit all of his faults, but I did expect something from him...some kind of guilt.

"Losing your mother was difficult. I always assumed we would grow old together. Maybe in your eyes, I'm already ancient, but I expected us to live longer than this. I assumed I would die first so I would never have to feel this kind of pain. She's been gone for two years, and it still hurts as much as the first day she left."

The room turned eerily silent as he shared his thoughts with me. There was no apology in his words, more of a justification, but it was still more than he'd ever revealed before. I knew he loved my mother because he wouldn't have lost his mind if that weren't the case.

"Time stopped that day. Everything stopped. I forgot who I was. I forgot how to live. All I cared about was killing whoever was responsible for her death...as if that might bring her back to life. Reality was unbearable, so I focused on my goals with precision. As a result...I forgot everything else. That includes you and Lily."

That was more than I'd expected him to say, even though it wasn't an apology. "I took a bullet for you, and you screamed at me."

He looked away, his eyes focusing on one of the paintings. "Because that bullet would have killed me...and I wanted to die."

My eyes dropped for a moment, saddened to hear how depressed my father was.

"Living without her is unbearable. I wish I'd died that day instead of her. I'd gladly take her place in a heartbeat. She's much stronger than I am, so she would have survived my passing..."

As a married man, I'd begun to look at life differently. I was a brand-new newlywed because I only recently started to take my marriage seriously, and I already couldn't imagine my life without her. I'd lost her once, and it was a difficult pill to swallow. I worked my ass off to get her back because bachelorhood was mundane and lonely. Now that I had her back, I never wanted to let her go... But someday we would part. I would either lose her or she would lose me. It was a terrifying thought.

It made me understand my father a little better.

He reached for his glass but didn't take a drink. "Did I tell you how I met your mother?"

I nodded. "In a coffee shop."

"True. But the reason we met was because our families asked us to. It wasn't an arranged marriage, but it was pretty close. I was a young man and enjoyed all the perks of being a wealthy bachelor. She was a beautiful woman who could have any man she wanted. Neither one of us was interested in settling down at the time. She was in her early twenties...very young. But when we met...we just knew. Our families were ecstatic that we tied the knot, and we lived a happy life together."

"I never knew that..."

"She didn't like to tell people that story. Made it seem less romantic."

Now I found it more romantic.

"When I think about how she died..." He took a deep breath, and his nostrils flared. His eyes drifted down to the table, his thoughts a million miles away. "It still haunts me. She's at peace, and I know she forgives me...but it still haunts me."

"It haunts me too..."

"Experiencing something traumatic like that breaks you. What would you have done if Kamikaze took Arwen away and did unspeakable things to her? Would you have gone home and returned to work like nothing ever happened?"

I would have lost my mind too. "You were the one who told

Kamikaze my marriage was a sham...so that almost did happen." He'd stabbed me in the back and took the coward's way out. It was despicable. The memory got me worked up all over again.

"Yes...I suppose."

"So you wanted him to do your dirty work because you were too much of a coward to do it yourself." Our conversation had been going somewhere for once, but my rage caused a bump in the road.

He raised his gaze and stared at me. "Your wife caught me off guard when she cornered me. I didn't appreciate that."

"Yes, she's smarter than you. Didn't realize you would take that so personally."

He took a drink. "If it weren't for me, she would still be living in that piece-of-shit apartment bedding pretty boys. I kept her legs closed and returned her to where she belonged."

My eyes narrowed as my body tensed. "Don't talk about her like that." She had bedded other men, but that was only because I'd bedded other women. It was a retaliation, not an impulse. "She left because I fucked up. I don't blame her for leaving."

"What did you do?"

I was surprised Arwen didn't tell him. "That's between us."

"Well, you wouldn't have gotten her back if it weren't for me. Don't forget that."

"I won't," I said. "Just like I won't forget when you encouraged Kamikaze to kidnap my wife and rape her." I should take the glass in front of me and smash it over his thick skull.

His eyes turned down once more. "I shouldn't have done that... It was impulsive."

"Cowardly. That's the word you're looking for."

"It worked out in the end."

I cocked my eyebrow. "I almost died. I had to point a gun to my head and pull the trigger over and over again. My brains almost exploded across that restaurant as my body thudded to the floor and created a huge pool of blood." I remembered exactly how Kamikaze looked when that bullet took him out of existence. It was messy and disgusting. It could have been me. "I called you before I left, and you didn't give a damn—about your own son." I'd come all the way here on Christmas Day when I should have been home with my wife. This man didn't deserve my time. He wasn't on his knees begging for forgiveness, so I was talking to a brick wall. Maybe he did lose his mind when he lost my mother —but that was no justification. I was hurt, still tender like a recent wound. It killed me to feel this kind of indifference from my own father, the man who raised me.

I came here in the hope of resolution, but now I was only reminded how worthless he was. My anger rose to rage, and when I hit my critical level, there was no chance of calming down. My hands pushed against the table as I shoved myself out of my seat. The chair flew back, and I prepared to storm out. "This was a waste of time. Goodbye, Caspian." I would never call him my father again because the title simply wasn't fitting anymore. I wasn't sure what he was. A stranger.

"Maverick."

Any other time, I would have stopped at his command like an obedient dog. Even when I was enraged, I could never ignore my father. It was disrespectful and strange. But those days were over —and I kept walking. It was time to walk out of that house and never come back. It was time to be with my real family.

I headed down the hall and approached the front door. To my surprise, I heard footsteps behind me.

"I did care, Maverick. Of course I did."

"Didn't seem like it." I reached the door and opened it. The second it was cracked, the cold draft blew into the house. There was no sign of rain or snow, but the cold and dry air was immediately harsh against my skin. I knew I was leaving my family's home for the last time—and I would never see it again.

"The reason you're alive is because of me."

Just when I was about to step out into the elements, I steadied myself and let those words sink in. My hand was still on the door, and I stared at my black car in the driveway. The wind was picking up, and the trees on the property were starting to sway. His words shouldn't entice me to stay, but now I couldn't leave. I turned back to him, hoping I wouldn't regret it.

"I had one of my men facilitate the game. He remembered where he put the bullet in the chamber and made sure you went first. When he flipped that coin into the air, he never showed either of you what it said—because he lied." His boots thudded against the floor as he slowly approached me, his shoulders not as powerful as they were when he'd first let me into the house. Now his weight sagged him down, made him droop toward the earth with age. "I made sure Kamikaze died and you lived. Like I would ever let anything happen to you."

Now I ignored the coldness on the front doorstep and locked eyes with my father. That afternoon was one of the most terrifying experiences of my life. While I'd kept a straight face for Arwen and Kamikaze, I was dying on the inside. At any moment, this life could have been over. "Why didn't you tell me?"

He shrugged slightly as he sighed under his breath.

"Because that would require you to admit that you cared?"

"Maybe..." It was the first time my father had chased me down so I wouldn't leave. It was the first time he'd stopped his psychological warfare. Now he was just a man...a father. Vulnerable and defenseless, he let himself be weak...even if it was short term.

In disbelief, I continued to stare at him. My father actually had done something on my behalf. During that conversation, he seemed so indifferent to my potential death that it numbed me down to the bone. "Why is that so difficult for you?"

"I don't know. Maybe because you remind me so much of your mother."

"I look nothing like her."

"But you have her spirit. You have her attitude, her strength. Whenever I look at you, it reminds me how I let her down, how she would give anything to stand where I am now so she could look at you. My family has been ripped apart...and it's all my fault. It's easier to stop feeling than to let that depression spread through your veins like a disease. She's dead because of me...and that truth has been very difficult for me to accept." He dropped his gaze and looked at the floor like he couldn't stand it anymore. Now he was just a broken man, not a crazy dictator. His armor had been shed and his weapons abandoned. There was no more fight in him.

My anger disappeared.

"I lost my mind because the pain was too difficult to swallow. It was self-preservation, the only way I could function. I focused on killing Ramon because I thought it would give me some kind of release...but it never did. I wanted to do the same to his wife and daughter because I had nothing else to do with my time, except sit with a drink in my hand and think about the terrible things I'd done. Getting angry with your wife and threatening to kill her gave me something else to focus on. It was better than actually accepting responsibility for all my wrongdoings."

It was the first time I'd really seen my father in two years. It was easy to forget how he used to be because that version of him seemed long gone. But here he was...still the same man I used to know. He was buried under guilt, pain, and remorse...but he was still there. "Lily and I lost her too. We needed you, especially her."

"I know..."

"Mom would be disappointed if she knew you'd been acting this way since she died."

"I think she does know. I think she's watching me now and wishing she could smack me upside the head. I was a terrible husband, and now I'm a terrible father. Your mother's greatest mistake was falling in love with me."

I remembered the way they used to kiss on the couch when they thought I wasn't looking, the way my father would carry anything remotely heavy so she wouldn't have to worry about it. I remembered the way he complimented her every time she got dressed up for a party. When I looked back on my parents' marriage, I remembered seeing two people in love. They rarely fought and worked equally at the relationship. My father never would have gotten involved with the underworld if he'd known it would cost him his wife's life. "If she had the choice to do it all over again, I'm sure she wouldn't hesitate. She wouldn't trade in that life for anything else in the world." Even if she'd known she would die a gruesome death, she never would have traded in being a mother to Lily and me, to being a wife to my father. She could have married someone else and lived a long and happy life...but she wouldn't have done it.

"You're probably right, but that doesn't make me feel better."

"You couldn't have known that was going to happen."

"I still should have done a better job protecting my family. I hope you learn from my mistakes."

I'd inherited a lot of things from my father, but recently, I'd only inherited his flaws. I became a reclusive bachelor who was incapable of feeling anything besides lust and thirst for booze. I had a wife who clearly adored me, but I'd never returned her affection until she was gone. I mirrored his foul mood and asshole attitude. It wasn't obvious to me until that moment. His depression had sunk into me and infected me like an illness. "I already have."

My father kept the distance between us and didn't try to embrace me. But he also didn't apologize. That seemed like something that would never happen because he was too stubborn.

But that was okay...because I got more than I'd ever expected. My father had been looking out for me when I didn't realize it, and that meant so much to me. It made me feel less alone in this world. "So...does that mean you'll stop threatening to kill my wife?"

He smiled at the cruel joke. "I suppose."

"She said you were never going to do it anyway."

"She's a smart woman. Reminds me of your mother."

She reminded me of her too...when she gave me thoughtful gifts, smiled at me like I was her whole world, and picked up my clothes off the floor and hung them over the back of the chair even though Abigail would take care of it the next day. "I was so pissed off when you made me marry her."

"But it was the best thing that ever happened to you, huh?"

"Yeah...it is."

"Arwen has bigger balls than you and me. When she set me up at the rehab center, I understood exactly who I was dealing with. I was annoyed she caught me off guard...but I also respected her for risking her safety to do something good for you. Telling Kamikaze was a mistake that never should have happened...but it led to his ultimate demise, so I guess it worked out."

"Yeah...I guess."

Now he stared at me like he didn't know what else to say.

I didn't have anything to say either. I needed time to process this lengthy conversation, to let the shock soak in. My father and I had made peace, and I could hardly believe it. I turned to the door and stepped out. "I guess I'll see you later, then."

"Yes, I suppose. Merry Christmas, son."

A hug didn't seem appropriate. Even when we were on good terms, we never did that sort of thing. But it felt strange just leaving after the intense moment we'd just shared. "Would you like to come over for dinner?" I didn't want my father to spend the holiday in our family home all alone. It might be weird to have him over for dinner, but it was better to offer than just to leave him there.

His eyes didn't blink as he stared at me, like he couldn't believe I'd extended such an offer. After everything he'd put me through, it was probably a surprise to get an invitation. I was even surprised I'd made the offer in the first place. He gave a slight nod. "If that's okay with your wife."

"She was the one who forced me to come in the first place. And now I understand why..."

He nodded. "I told her about Kamikaze. I'm surprised she didn't tell you herself."

I already knew why. "She wanted me to hear it from you."

17

ARWEN

Maverick was gone for a long time, so I took that as a good sign.

Unless one of them killed the other.

With those two men, I really had no idea what might happen. Maverick had too big of a heart to kill his father, but he'd been putting up with a lot of bullshit for a long time. He might snap and do something he regretted. Caspian was harmless. He wouldn't have protected his son if he'd wanted him dead.

Hours later, Maverick's footsteps were audible in the hallway. The sound was distinct because it sounded like a man's approach, not Abigail's light footsteps. I was sitting on his bed with the fireplace in full flame, the picture of us together on my nightstand. I assumed I would move in to his bedroom even though we'd never actually talked about it. But if he loved me, why would he want me anywhere else?

Maverick walked inside and immediately shed his dark coat. It slid down his powerful arms before he tossed it over the back of the chair. His dark eyes were set on me, impossible to read because he always looked like a blank page in a book.

"You're alive... That's a good sign. Is he?"

He nodded then approached the bed. He took a seat at the edge, his gaze forward so I could only see the side of his face. His hands rested on his thighs as he stared toward the bathroom. "Yeah."

"Then that must have been a good conversation."

"It went better than I thought it would. He didn't apologize...not that I expected him to. I hoped it would happen, dreamed it would happen, but that will always be just a fantasy. My father is too proud to say those words...even if he should."

"Then what did he say instead?"

He sighed before he answered. "That he loved my mother with everything he had...and losing her was agonizing. He wishes it'd been him instead of her. He lost sight of everything after she was gone, drowning in guilt and depression."

"So it was an explanation."

He shrugged. "I guess. He was difficult to talk to in the beginning. I got so angry with him that I stormed out. When he called my name, I didn't even bother turning around. But then he told me he rigged the roulette so I would win..." His eyes fell to the floor, and he turned stony as he became lost in thought. He'd had to deal with the fear of his father despising him, and now he realized his father actually did care about him. It was a lot to soak in.

"He cares about you, Maverick. He just struggles to show it."

"Yeah...I guess you're right. I guess you've always been right."

My hand moved to his back, and I gently rubbed his strong muscles, moving from the back of his shoulder down to his hips. Maverick never used to confide in me, but now were confidants to each other. "Did he say anything else?"

"It's hard to look at Lily and me because he knows my mother misses us, would do anything to look at our faces every single day. He feels responsible for her death, so he pushes us away. It's not right, but I get it."

"Now that it's been a few years and he's lightened up, maybe he'll change. Just the fact that you had this conversation indicates he's changed."

"I guess."

My fingers moved into his hair next. "Do you feel better?"

After a long pause of indifference, he nodded. "Yeah...a bit. I really thought my father hated me."

"He never did."

"And I really thought he hated you, but I think he's fond of you."

My fingers left his hair then traveled down his arm until they returned to the bed. "I don't think he ever wanted to kill me, but I don't think he liked me much."

"He respects you. That's as close as you'll get."

"That's interesting. I feel like all I've done is insult him."

"That's probably why he respects you. You aren't afraid of him."

"If he was someone I should be afraid of, I would be. Kamikaze terrified me. Your father was a wannabe bully. He was just a broken man who needed a wake-up call."

"Then maybe he feels gratitude toward you."

"Maybe," I whispered. "I'm just glad the two of you could connect in some way. A father and son shouldn't be this distant from each other. Sometimes resentment festers into rage and you forget you're family...and you need help rectifying that situation. There are a lot of things I don't like about your father, but when he told me what he did for you with Kamikaze, I knew he would do anything to protect you. It made me forgive him for the things he said to me, for the way he treated you. Sometimes it's hard to forgive people who've wronged you, but you have to start somewhere."

"I told him you forced me to go over there."

"He probably assumed that on his own."

He gave a faint chuckle. "Yeah." It turned quiet as he stared at the floor, still reflecting on the conversation he'd had with his father.

"You think he'll talk to Lily?"

"I'd be surprised if he didn't. She's the one who needs his support right now. By the way...I invited him for dinner."

That was the moment I knew everything would be okay. It may not be perfect. There probably would be a lot of tense exchanges across the table and awkward stares, but at least we would all be together. It would never be perfect, and we couldn't forget what happened in the past, but it would start to get better...slowly. "That's great."

"You don't mind?"

"Not at all. I'm very happy he's coming."

"Even though he threatened to kill you so many times?"

"No. Those were empty threats. I have an extra box of chocolates, so I'll give that to him as a present."

"I'm sure he doesn't expect anything."

"Well, I can't eat them. I've already eaten too many holiday treats already. And it's the gesture that counts."

He finally turned his gaze on me, his eyes softer than I'd ever seen them. His hand moved to my thigh, and he leaned in close to me, like he might kiss me. "Thank you for making this happen. Wouldn't have been possible without you."

I cupped my husband's face and looked deep into his beautiful eyes. "I will always take care of you...just as you'll always take care of me."

MAVERICK WORE the collared shirt I got him for Christmas, and of course, he looked stunning in it. It was the perfect color for the holiday, the perfect cut for his sexy physique. I wore a long-sleeved red dress and heels. We entered the formal dining room and shared a bottle of wine. Neither one of us made conversation because we were both listening for the sound of the door.

It was the first time I would dine with my father-in-law. I suspected it was the first time Maverick would spend the evening with his own father since his mother died. It was a tense Christmas, but I wouldn't have it any other way.

I wished my own father were here to spend it with me.

The front door opened and closed, and then Abigail escorted him to the dining room. "It's nice to see you, Mr. DeVille. May I take your coat?"

"Please."

Maverick sighed before he rose to his feet, like he was dreading this even though he was the one who had extended the invitation.

I got to my feet too. "It'll be alright."

A glass of wine was on the table, so he grabbed it and took a long drink. His sobriety was only a memory the second his father walked in the door.

Caspian entered the dining room a moment later, his eyes immediately going to the decorated Christmas tree in the corner. As if it brought memories into his mind, a soft smile entered his lips before he addressed his son. "I haven't eaten anything today, so I'm excited for this." He extended his hand to shake Maverick's.

It was probably too soon for a hug, so Maverick took his grip, and they completed the handshake like gentlemen. "Abigail is an amazing cook, so I'm sure it'll be worth it." Maverick mirrored his slight smile, and it seemed genuine. He was nervous just seconds ago, but seeing his father enter the room with no pretense of hostility calmed him down.

Caspian turned to me next. He kept a foot in between us and didn't extend his hand to shake mine, probably deeming it too masculine. "Mrs. DeVille, nice to see you again."

"Arwen is fine."

He nodded then took a seat at the head of the table.

Right on cue, Abigail filled his wineglass and served the meal. A Christmas turkey was placed in the center, along with stuffing, potatoes, steamed carrots, and freshly baked rolls.

Maverick reached for the food first and made his own plate.

Caspian and I followed his lead.

Like a normal family on a normal Christmas, we dined together.

Caspian drank the wine without complaint and didn't ask for scotch. He didn't make conversation as he ate his food, preferring silence to mundane conversation. He probably didn't know what to say, and if he did something, he might regret it.

I stared at Maverick because I didn't know what else to do.

Just like his father, Maverick had his eyes downcast as he ate.

I cleared my throat to finally address Caspian. "So—"

"I'm sorry for all the death threats I made." He addressed the elephant in the room when no one else did. He grabbed his linen napkin and wiped the crumbs from his lips before he kept speaking. "Truth is, I didn't know what else to do with myself. Since you disobeyed me, I thought your actions should be punished. But at the end of the day, it really doesn't make a difference. Whether those women lived or died, it wouldn't have helped me sleep better at night."

"It would have made you sleep worse. I didn't disobey you—I helped you." I hated the use of that word, like I had to listen to his rules because I was an inferior woman. I didn't appreciate the way Caspian spoke about obedience, but I should focus on getting along with him, not insulting him.

Caspian watched me with cold eyes but didn't make any threats. "The only reason I married you off to my son was because I needed that information about Ramon. I had to kill him to get some peace. Watching the light leave his eyes did give me some sense of satisfaction. My wife deserved revenge, and I wasn't going to stop until she got it. But something very good came out of that because you make my son happy. You're good for him."

"Thank you…" My fingertips rested on the stem of my wineglass.

"Most people wouldn't have had the strength to confront me like that. And you're so smart that it's concerning. I think you'll teach my son a few things."

"Maverick is a very capable man," I said loyally. "He's taught me a lot…"

Caspian gave a slight smile. "Then you're perfect for each other."

I took a drink of my wine and looked at my husband across the table. "I couldn't agree more."

AT THE END of the night, we walked Caspian to the door.

I held out the box of chocolates to him. "Merry Christmas, Caspian." It wasn't much, just a cheap box of caramel chocolates I picked up while shopping, but it was probably the only gift he would get this year.

He took it in his large hands and stared at the red bow on top. With a moment of hesitation, he examined the box like he couldn't identify what it was. Then a small smile came over his lips, and he raised his gaze to meet mine. "Thank you. And thank you for putting up with my son...and me."

"Yes, you're both a handful," I said with a chuckle. "But you both have qualities that I like."

"I can see that in Maverick...not so much in myself." He tucked the box of chocolates under his arm then said goodbye to his son. "Thank you for inviting me. This was nice. Much better than sitting at home alone."

"Yeah." Maverick kept his hands in his pockets like he didn't want to give or receive affection. "It was nice."

After staring at his son for a while, Caspian opened the door and stepped out into the darkness. He got into his car, started the engine, and then drove away. His red taillights were visible until he reached the gate and turned onto the main road.

Maverick shut the door and bolted the lock. Like he'd been holding his breath for the last few hours, he released the air stuffed in his lungs and let his shoulders relax.

"That went well."

"Yeah, it did." He leaned against the door with his hand on the knob. "I was waiting for it to go to shit any moment."

To me, it seemed like the road would be a smooth one. It might not be perfect and it would take a long time for trust to be rebuilt, but at least they were on the right track. "I don't think you have to worry about that. I know it's hard to let your guard down, but I don't think your father has a trick up his sleeve. The last two years have been hard for you, so I understand if your guard stays up for a while. Rome wasn't built in a day."

"You're a lot more pragmatic about this than I am."

"That's because I haven't been his victim for two years."

"He was an ass to you."

I shrugged. "I have a pretty thick skin."

"No. It's soft, beautiful, and kissable." He pushed off the door and came close to me, his arms circling my waist as he forgot about his father. When his eyes settled on me, he didn't think about anything else besides us. "I have a surprise for you."

"You already got me a great present yesterday."

"I know, but I have something better for you. Want to see it?"

I already had the perfect husband. What more could I possibly want? "You know I won't stop thinking about it until you do."

"Alright." He took my hand and guided me up the three flights of stairs until we entered his bedroom.

When I walked inside, I expected to see a wrapped present on the bed or a gown lying across the back of the chair. He usually bought me clothes and jewelry, and he nailed it every time. I stepped inside and took a look around, not seeing anything out of the ordinary. "Where is it?"

He opened the door to the walk-in closet. "Here."

When I looked inside, I saw all my clothes hanging on the rack opposite his. My heels and shoes were placed in the cubbies, and there was a box that held all of my jewelry.

"And here." He moved to the bathroom and showed me all my hair supplies sitting on the counter. My makeup, brushes, and everything else I used was there, along with a fresh arrangement of winter flowers. "Last but not least..." He walked to the other side of the bed then nodded to the nightstand.

It took me two seconds to figure out what he'd done. He'd had his servants move everything from my bedroom to his while we had dinner, officially moving me in to his bedroom. Our bedroom.

I went to the nightstand and opened the drawer. The little things I had tucked away were there, from hair ties, to old pictures, to miscellaneous things I didn't know what to do with. "This felt like my bedroom a long time ago..." I shut the drawer and turned around. "I'd love to live with you, but I have to warn you—" I shut my mouth when I noticed him on the rug on one knee. A brown box was in his hand, and he gripped the velvet-covered container like he was about to open it at any second.

I was already married to this man. We'd already had a wedding, already had a future together. But we'd never had a proposal— and I couldn't believe I was getting one now. It felt right the second I looked at him, the moment my brain caught up with my heart. My hands automatically cupped my face like this was a dream come true, like I hadn't seen him wear his wedding ring every single day for the last few months.

With his eyes glued to mine, he popped open the box. The same princess cut diamond I'd been wearing for almost a year sat inside, just as beautiful and shiny as the first day he gave it to me. I'd grown attached to that ring that moment I saw it even though it took much longer to become attached to him. "Will you marry me, Sheep?"

It was a comical question to ask considering I was already married to him, but I'd never been asked that question before, so my lips threw out the answer my soul wanted to give. "Yes."

He pulled the ring out of the box and slipped it onto my finger.

Now that I was reacquainted with my ring, I never wanted to take it off. I'd felt so lost without it. Even when I'd first left him, I still wore my ring every single day. The only reason I took it off was because he came after me and reminded me of what he'd done. I stared at the beautiful diamonds on my left hand and felt my soul start to throb at the connection I felt immediately. Our marriage hadn't always been perfect...but I wouldn't have it any other way. "I love it. And I love you."

He rose to his feet and slid his arms around my waist. "I know you do." His lips found my hairline, and he kissed me on the forehead as his hands tightened around my hips. He slowly tugged me closer into him until our foreheads were pressed together.

My arms rested on his, and I closed my eyes as I felt everything fall into place. I fell in love with my husband and couldn't imagine being with any other man. He was strong, smart, sexy as hell, and the best lover I'd ever had. He was my protector, my friend, and everything that I would ever need. There was a gaping hole in my chest that my late father left behind, but Maverick filled it so nicely. Now I didn't need anything else but the man who'd given me his last name.

"Will you marry me again?"

I opened my eyes and lifted my gaze to meet his.

"Put on a wedding dress, exchange vows, and live happily ever after."

"You want to do that again?" My words came out as a whisper because I was surprised by the romantic gesture. He'd already married me once. I didn't see why he would want to do it again.

"Yes. But do it right this time."

"It's almost January..."

"We'll go somewhere warm for the honeymoon."

We didn't have a honeymoon the first time because neither one of us was attracted to the other. We'd both viewed that day as an obligation, something we wanted to get past as quickly as possible. Then we'd stayed on opposite sides of the house and barely interacted as friends.

"Not that we'll be outside much..." He wore that charming grin that made me fall in love with him all over again.

"I'd love that."

"You already have a dress, and I have a suit. I don't think we need much else."

"No...but I'm not taking off my ring again."

"Neither will I. We'll just renew our vows."

"And where will we go on our honeymoon?"

"Wherever you want."

"Somewhere tropical would be nice..."

"Have you ever been to the Maldives?"

I'd barely left Italy. I took the train through France and the rest of Europe, but I'd never ventured farther than that. The warmest place I'd ever been was Greece at the height of summer. "No."

"Then that's where we'll go. We'll have our own bungalow over the water, order room service for all our meals, and make some babies."

"Babies, huh? Didn't realize you wanted a family."

He shrugged. "I'm not repulsed by the idea anymore."

I chuckled. "That's romantic..."

"Missing my mother and being estranged from my father makes me want to have a family of my own."

"Well...I'm not looking to be a mother right now. Let's not forget I'm almost a decade younger than you. Maybe we could wait a couple of years?"

He didn't show a hint of disappointment. His eyes burned with affection, and his lips rose in a slight smile. "We'll wait however long you want to."

"Besides." I pulled him closer and pressed our heads together. "I want to enjoy you a little longer..."

18

MAVERICK

It was a frosty afternoon in Florence because the winter season was particularly cold that year. A clear sky was just as formidable as rain and wind because it was so damn cold. Most of the people on the street wore gloves, but I ran ten degrees warmer than everyone else, so I didn't bother.

I entered the rehab facility and passed the check-in desk. I wanted to tell Lily everything that had happened with Father, but I didn't think it should be done over the phone. Since I was getting married...again...I hoped she'd be there for the ceremony. It was more important than the first one anyway.

I passed the dining room, and that's when I stopped in my tracks.

Lily sat in the booth with my father across from her, two coffees in front of them. Still steaming but untouched, they acted as placeholders to distract from the tension. Lily was slumped forward with her head slightly down because she was unable to meet my father's gaze.

My father seemed remorseful...even a little ashamed.

I stood there and tried to decide what to do. It seemed wrong to disturb them when they were in such deep conversation. My father probably had shown up there to apologize, and that was exactly what my sister needed. She was in rehab because she felt so lost in the real world. Making up with our father was probably what she needed to stand on her own two feet again.

Just when I was about to turn away, my father looked up and noticed me.

Our eyes locked, and I stopped breathing altogether. It was strange to look at him without seeing that hostility rise into his features. He always used to look at me like I was a bitter disappointment, a borderline enemy. But that look wasn't forthcoming. Now he just looked like my father...and nothing else.

Then he nodded for me to come over.

I walked to their table and looked at my sister. Old tearstains were visible down her cheeks, and her eyes were puffy like a waterfall had recently cascaded from her eyes. It took her a few seconds for her to lift her gaze and meet my stare. "Hey, Maverick."

"Can I join you?"

She nodded.

I took a seat beside my sister and felt the weight of the moment crush me. It was the first time my family had been together since my mother passed away. It was the first time the three of us were under the same roof, as a family. It wasn't the same as it used to be, not when my mother's laugh wasn't there to fill the pockets of silence. There was a deep hole inside of every one of us without her presence. But at least we were together now...and I was happy.

"DAMN, I didn't expect to see you with a drink in your hand so soon." Kent sat across from me in the booth at the back of the bar, his long-sleeved shirt covered by his gray blazer. His skin was fairer every time I saw him because the sun wasn't there to kiss it a golden brown.

The scotch was in front of me, but I took my time drinking it and refrained from ordering another. Now that I understood what my limit was, I knew I could drink the way I used to—but not a sip more. That was one of the most humiliating nights of my life, and I didn't want to repeat it. My wife would still love me the next morning. She would still take care of me throughout the night. But I still didn't want to repeat it anyway. "I'm getting my feet back in the water."

"You aren't you without scotch in your system, so I'm glad to see it. And since you have a wife to come pick you up when you get carried away, even better. You aren't my problem."

"Good thing we're friends," I teased.

He held up his glass and tapped it to mine.

I returned the gesture. "And assholes."

He chuckled then took a drink. "So, you and your dad are square?"

"Well, we're starting to be square. We have a long way to go."

"At least he doesn't want to kill your or your hot wife."

I was about to drink from my glass but shot him a glare instead.

"What?" he asked incredulously. "You didn't give her the time of day in the beginning. I was the one who reminded you that she was sex on legs, and that's when you finally woke up. So, you're welcome."

I let it slide. "She and I are getting married tomorrow."

He almost spat out the drink he'd just took. He managed to keep it locked behind his lips until he could swallow it and force it down his throat. He wiped his forearm across his mouth to catch the drops that escaped. "Back up. Did you get divorced?"

"No. But we're doing another ceremony."

"You haven't even been married for a year," he said incredulously. "What's with the fairy-tale shit?"

"The first wedding didn't mean anything to either of us. She was coerced and so was I. But now that we want to be together—"

"So, you finally admit you love this woman?"

When I said it to her on Christmas, I didn't think twice about it. She'd looked so beautiful under the Christmas tree, the lights reflecting in her bright eyes. Her gift was thoughtful, showing her affection that had never disappeared, even after the terrible things I'd done. It was nice...just to sit there with her, to have someone to spend the holiday with. Before I knew it, the words were flying out of my mouth and exploding into the air. "Yeah."

Instead of teasing me, Kent gave me a smile. "Good. Finally got your head on straight. Women like that don't pop up often."

"Sounds like you have a crush on my wife."

He shrugged. "She got a sister?"

I rolled my eyes. "Only child."

"Damn." He slammed down his drink playfully. "If her parents can make beautiful babies like that, they should have made more."

"You'll find someone, Kent. You can have whoever you want."

"But I don't want just anybody. Sabrina was a good lay, by the way. But she's totally a bitch."

"Oh, I know," I said with a chuckle. "It's a turn-off to see a woman go after a married man."

"Never cared about that before."

"Well, I care now." I'd never respected the institution of marriage until I'd participated in my own. Then I started to understand the depth of love, the real meaning of commitment. There was nothing stronger than the love between a husband and wife. The fact that someone would come in between that...was disgusting. If another man tried to steal my wife, I'd be devastated.

"So, is this more of a vow renewal?"

"I guess. But it feels like a wedding to us."

"She going to wear her old wedding dress?"

I nodded. "And I'll wear my suit."

"Where are you going to do this?"

"At the house."

"Like, in the middle of winter?"

"Yep."

Kent took another drink. "Shit, it will be cold."

"Yep. So we'd both better drink a lot."

"We?" he asked. "I'm coming to this thing."

"I would hope so. You're my best man."

For a short span of time, he dropped his joking manner and allowed himself to actually feel the moment. His eyes softened, and an unstoppable smile spread across his lips. "Even though I think your wife is hot?"

I shrugged. "Everyone thinks my wife is hot."

"I'll probably think she's sexy in her wedding dress."

"That makes two of us."

He held up his glass to mine again. "Then I'd be honored, man."

"Me too."

WE GOT lucky with the weather. Not a cloud in the sky. It hadn't rained in a week, so the soil wasn't muddy. The sunlight provided an extra few degrees of temperature, but the lack of a cloud bank made it considerably colder.

But that didn't dull the warm feeling inside my chest.

I woke up that morning next to my wife and then got ready to marry her again.

Not a bad way to start my day.

It only took me thirty minutes to get ready, so I stayed in the dining room downstairs with Kent and my family so Arwen could take her time getting dressed. I hoped she wouldn't let the memory of her parents overshadow her happiness. Obviously, she would be sad they both weren't there to witness this important event in her life, but I hoped she would know they were watching anyway.

Now that Lily had settled things with my father, she'd left the rehab center and moved into my apartment in Florence. I never used it, so she may as well take advantage of the vacancy. She was at the house now, wearing a long-sleeved dress with her hair done in curls.

I took a seat and stared at the bottle of scotch in the center of the table.

Kent got my attention from across the table and mouthed to me, "Your sister is cute."

I rolled my eyes.

My father noticed what Kent said, so he gave him the death stare.

Kent brushed it off by refilling his glass of scotch. "So, nervous?"

"No." I drummed my fingers against the table. "I feel like I'm getting a second chance to make this right. When we first got married, it was a terrible day for us both. It took a long time for us to respect each other, to tolerate each other. But now, I'm already in love, and I'm looking forward to the future."

"Wow, my brother isn't an asshole after all." Lily smiled at me, telling me she was teasing me.

"Not anymore, at least," I replied.

"Nah, he's still a dick if you ask me." Kent took another drink from his glass.

My father sat there, still like a statue and quiet like death. "Arwen is a lucky girl. And you're a very lucky man."

I still wasn't used to compliments from him. Hard to believe they were real.

A few minutes later, heels echoed on the hardwood floor before Arwen made her entrance. In the same white wedding dress she wore on our wedding day, she looked just as beautiful.

Actually, she looked more beautiful.

I stared at her for a couple seconds, treasuring the way the sunlight hit her so perfectly. It made her dress glow and her happiness shine. Her hair was done the way I liked, and her dark eyeshadow made her look mysterious and sexy. I'd taken her to bed many times, but now it felt like it never happened. Now it felt like the first time all over again.

Everyone else was quiet, speechless from her appearance.

I got out of the chair and walked toward her, buttoning my suit jacket as I went. It was the only time I could recall feeling nervous in my adult life. Even when I was gambling with my life in Russian roulette, my stomach didn't feel quite as unbalanced as this. My nerves didn't fire off in trepidation and excitement. My eyes stayed on her as I walked to her, appreciating the sight of her in her wedding dress for the first time. I'd stared at her as she'd come down the aisle, but I'd never truly cared what I was looking at. But now it was special to me... Everything was special.

My initial instinct was to bend my neck and kiss her, but I'd have to save that for later.

She smiled when she watched my head dip down toward her. "It'll have to wait."

"You know I'm not patient."

She rose on her tiptoes and used my arms for balance. Then she placed a kiss on my cheek. "Then that will have to do."

My arm secured around her waist, and I walked her outside into the cold. We were getting married under the same tree where we got married last time, at the edge of the front of my property. "Would you like my jacket?"

"No." Her happiness seemed to be keeping her warm.

The five of us moved to the tree at the edge of the grass along the stone pathway. The priest who married us last time was there, holding the bible in his hands at his waist. He looked exactly the same, wearing a thick coat with glasses.

The ceremony didn't happen the same way it had last time. She didn't walk down the aisle to me. There were no guests except for my family. It was just us two, so we didn't need any more.

Kent stood beside me while my sister and father filled up the rest of the space. They were quiet as they watched me get married a second time. Lily hadn't been there the first time, but it didn't matter. That ceremony wasn't as important as this one.

I took Arwen's hands in mine and squeezed her fingertips.

She stared at me with the same look she gave me every day, a look that said she loved me without the use of words. Almost a year ago, she was in tears, knowing her father only had weeks to live and she was marrying a stranger she didn't even like. But now, everything was different. She was happy to be there, happy to squeeze my fingers in return.

I'd never imagined a day like this, a moment when I would face a woman and want to spend my life with her. My moodiness had dissolved, and now I felt optimistic about the future. This woman put my family back together...put me back together.

The priest began the ceremony, reading a section of the bible then proceeding forward. We didn't say our own vows last time, just made it cut-and-dried, but now we wanted to share our hearts.

"Maverick," the priest said. "You first."

I'd scribbled a few notes in my bedroom but didn't bring the paper with me. "I never cared about being a good husband or making you happy. I didn't appreciate you when every other man in the world would kill to make you his wife. That was how depressed I was, unable to feel anything going on around me. But you fixed me when I didn't realize I was broken. You made me whole when I realized I was incomplete. I never thought I'd actually want to be married to someone for the rest of my life, to have one woman in my life every single day. But you've made me fall so deeply in love with you, I can't imagine my life any other way. I wasn't good to you before, but now I promise to be the husband you deserve, to be faithful to you every day until my heart stops beating. I promise to protect you with my life. I promise to be a good father to our children. I promise to be whatever you want me to be...because I never want to lose you."

She blinked her eyes a few times to stop the tears, but then she couldn't hold them back. Her eyes grew wet, and a few tears streaked through her makeup and formed tiny rivers down her cheeks. Even with slightly smeared makeup and wet eyes, she was still the most desirable woman in the world. Anytime her tears appeared, I thought of the way she came when we were in bed together...and then my thoughts ran rampant. She controlled her emotions well enough to speak, and then she said her vows to me. "Maverick, I despised you when I became your wife..."

Kent, Lily, and my father all laughed.

A small smile was still on my lips. "Yeah...I know."

"You were moody, argumentative, and just a jackass. Anytime I tried to start a conversation, you were so cold. It made me feel so isolated when I had no one for comfort. But then all of that started to change when you showed your true colors. You were my rock when the worst things happened to me. You were my voice when I couldn't speak, my legs when I couldn't walk. You got me through my darkest hour. You became my closest friend. I never thought I would actually start to like my husband, but as time passed...I slowly fell in love with you. With every passing day, that feeling became stronger and stronger. Then I was so desperately in love with you that I couldn't imagine loving another man all my life. You weren't what I pictured in a husband, but you're exactly what I want. I couldn't imagine spending the rest of my life with anyone else, couldn't imagine having children with anyone else. You're all that I'll ever need, Maverick. I feel so lucky to be Mrs. DeVille."

The avalanche of compliments crushed me, and I couldn't believe the source was her beautiful mouth. This woman loved me despite my flaws, forgave me despite my sins. She loved me for me...and that meant the world to me. I was a difficult man who had mood swings that could be triggered at any moment, but she was patient and understanding. She saw the good in all the bad.

The priest finished the ceremony. "Maverick, do you take this woman to be your lawfully wedded wife—"

"I do." I blurted out the answer before he could even finish. I didn't want to waste another second holding my breath when I wanted to release the truth into the sky.

She smiled, her eyes still wet.

"And do you, Arwen, take this man—"

"I do."

I smiled in return.

"Then by the power vested in me, I pronounce you husband and wife."

Kent and my father applauded while Lily threw rose petals into the air.

My arms circled Arwen's waist, and I pulled her close to me so I could kiss her as my wife, to kiss her the way I should have on our wedding day. My arms locked around her back, and I crushed her into my chest, never wanting to let her go. My mouth found hers, and I kissed my wife, our lips landing like two sets of pillows. Soft and sexy, her mouth was the perfect oasis for my tongue. I kissed her with more passion than our last ceremony, my hand sliding into her hair as I disregarded the people staring at us. I kissed my wife how I wanted to because she was my wife...and I could do whatever I wanted.

Her returned affection was just as magical.

When I found the courage to pull away, I rested my forehead against hers and stared into her eyes. It was my job to take care of her, but she was the one who took care of me. She was the one who brought out the best in me, made me realize I was a good man after all. We would balance each other until time ran out. "Are you ready for our honeymoon?"

"You know I packed three days ago."

I grabbed her hand and turned to my family. "Thanks for coming...but we have somewhere to be."

"What?" Kent asked. "We aren't going to cut some cake? Dance a little?"

"Pictures?" Lily asked.

"No." I shook my father's hand then hugged my sister. "We have enough wedding pictures." I turned to Kent and shook his hand.

He waggled his eyebrows at me. "Have fun on your honeymoon. Hopefully, you come back."

I smiled. "I might not. And that would be okay because I hate your ugly face."

"Whoa...that's how you talk to your best man?"

"It is when you won't stop checking out my wife."

He shrugged. "Good point."

When I turned back to my wife, I saw her hugging my father.

I hadn't seen my father hug anyone besides my mother...and that was two years ago. Stunned, I watched him embrace her then whisper something in her ear. When they broke apart, he patted her shoulder and gave her a slight smile.

Did that just happen?

Arwen came back to me and grabbed my hand. "Alright, I'm ready to go. When does our flight leave?"

Hand in hand, we walked back to the house. "I can't believe my father hugged you."

"Before you freak out, just remember he's a lot like you. He's rough around the edges but soft on the inside. He's like a caramel chocolate."

"What did he say to you?"

She looked at me, a knowing smile on her lips. "That's between me and my father-in-law."

"You really aren't going to share?" I asked, surprised she would keep such a secret from me.

"I'll tell you on our honeymoon. How about that?"

"Alright...even though I won't be in the mood for talking." We approached the hired SUV waiting for us. Our suitcases were already stuffed in the back, and we were ready for our week-long vacation in the Maldives.

"Should we change first?"

"We can change on the plane."

"That's gonna be hard with those little bathrooms."

"My bathrooms aren't little."

She stared at me with an eyebrow raised. "*Your* bathrooms?"

"I have my own plane. I never mentioned that?"

"Uh, no."

"Well, I guess you know now." I opened the back door for her.

"I've never been on a private plane."

"First time for everything."

She scooted into the back seat, and I sat beside her.

The driver pulled away and circled the roundabout as he headed for the main road.

Arwen sat in the middle of the back seat and tucked her arm

through mine. She leaned toward me and rested her head on my shoulder, her white dress taking up most of the back of the vehicle. Her brilliant wedding ring reflected the winter sun, and she got some of her foundation on the material of my suit.

I turned my head toward her and pressed a kiss to her forehead as we drove away.

"You're the best husband anyone could ask for," she whispered, her fingers squeezing my arm through my sleeve.

I kissed her forehead again, my hand moving to her thigh. "You made me the best husband anyone could ask for...which makes you the best wife."

EPILOGUE

ARWEN

EVEN THOUGH THE PRIVATE ISLAND IN THE MALDIVES WAS beautiful, with gorgeous beaches, nice restaurants, and a walking path that displayed beautiful views all around us, we stayed in our private bungalow and hardly ever left.

It was all about making love and ordering room service.

That was fine with me.

We had a secluded deck directly over the water with our own pool. When we weren't between the sheets, we were lounging in the sun with drinks in our hands, watching the sunset every night without a care in the world.

"It's beautiful here." I stood at the edge of the pool and looked over the side so I could see the ocean water below. It was shallow, full of small sharks, stingrays, and little fish. "What if we never go home and just stay here forever?"

He came to my side with a drink in his hand, standing in his swim trunks with a muscled chest. "We could."

"It is really cold back at home…"

"Another good point."

"Abigail can take a vacation."

"Nah. She'll be cleaning that house nonstop anyway. She's a hard worker. That's why I let her mouth off to me sometimes."

I chuckled. "You let her mouth off because you know she's right."

He shrugged. "Maybe."

I set my drink down and sat on the edge of the pool. The water ran a little warm from being exposed to the sun all day, so it felt like bathwater. With the sun setting over the horizon, a cool breeze came across the ocean and brushed through my hair. It was such a relief to feel the humidity stick to my skin and make it shine. I preferred summer over winter in any contest.

He came to my side and joined me. "So, what did he say?"

"You're on your honeymoon, but you're thinking about your father?"

"I'm just curious. I've never seen him embrace someone like that."

When Caspian hugged me but only shook his son's hand, I was just as perplexed. This man threatened to kill me on several occasions, so it was unbelievable that we'd ever buried the hatchet. But somehow, we did. He was a bitter and mean man, and what he needed was compassion and kindness. It was the perfect antidote to most problems. "Alright, you really want to know?"

"Yes."

"He said I was part of the family now, which means he'd do anything for me at any time. He said I was a daughter to him... and that his wife would have loved me."

Maverick stared at me for a while, at a loss for words. "Yes, she would have..."

"I know it's hard to see right now, but your father is a good man.

It's just taking him some time to get there. I was patient with you, so you should be patient with him."

Maverick was quiet once again, processing all of his emotions. "That was a nice thing he said to you."

"Yeah...he does have a heart under all that bullshit," I said with a chuckle. "Just like his son."

"Yes, we're two sensitive assholes." A slight smile formed on his lips. "I hated my father because of his behavior, but I never realized we were exactly the same. Everything that I am...comes from him."

"I don't know about that, but I see what you mean."

His arm draped over my shoulders, and he brought me close to him as we both looked at the dying light on the horizon. "So... how many kids do you want?"

"I thought we weren't starting a family for a couple years."

"I know. But I'm curious."

"Two," I answered. "You?"

"Two is perfect. And it's good you don't want to have kids right away. We need as much practice as possible."

I leaned into him and chuckled. "I think we're pretty good at it already."

"We could always be better." His hand moved to the back of my head, and he brought me in for a kiss. Like any other time he kissed me, it seemed like he wanted me more and more. He fell more in love with me every passing day, every passing week.

And I was falling in love with him more with every passing second.

I was falling in love with my husband...my wolf.

Keep reading for a sneak peek at my new series.

WIFE

I was twenty-one when the gypsy read my future:

As punishment for your crimes, you will only love one woman...but she'll never love you back.

I didn't believe a word of it.

Until I met Sofia Romano almost ten years later.

I fell hard for this woman. Would die for this woman.

But she left me.

Now years have passed and Sofia needs a husband. Her father is gone and her mother is trying to marry her off to a man that can protect their family, protect their company.

She's looking for someone powerful.

Check.

Someone rich.

Check.

Someone handsome.

Double check.

Now it's my chance to have the only woman I've ever loved...and I'll make sure she feels the same way.

I have a lifetime to make that happen.

TEASER OF WIFE

Prologue

Marrakech, Morocco

Hades

The bazaar was on fire.

Black cobras hissed at their masters when they heard the sound of the whip, men bravely shoved blades down their throats for entertainment, and gypsies danced for coins. When your donation wasn't generous enough, they sunk behind you and picked your pockets—taking what they deserved.

It was one hell of a place to celebrate my twenty-first birthday.

Damien walked beside me, a cigar sitting in his mouth. When a group of pretty girls passed, he gave them mere seconds of his attention before he moved onto the next sight. Now he stared at a camel being led away by its master. "What should we do now? Get a rug and take it home?"

"Rugs are nice." I liked Morocco because of the chaos. This city was unpredictable, from the dangerous route to the Atlas Mountains and the constant bomb checks under vehicles anytime you drove onto public property. It was a different kind of place, beautiful but unsteady.

"I'd rather spend my money on pussy—but not take it with me."

The brothels here were exciting—and dirt cheap. "Later." We spent the afternoon drinking, smoking, and exploring everything this city had to offer. It was a short flight away from Florence and an extreme change of scenery.

Damien sighed in dismay at my response. Of all the things he loved in life, pussy was his favorite. Booze and cigars came into a close second. But something changed his demeanor when he turned his head and examined the bright purple tent behind the vase stand. "Fortune reader...that's interesting."

"Is it?" The practice was nonsense, just a way to take your money then laugh at you on your way out.

"I've never done it before. Let's check it out." Damien sucked in one last puff before he threw his cigar on the ground and stomped on it. The ash squished under his shoe, adding to the other filth on the ground.

"You've got to be kidding me."

"What's the harm? We've got nothing else to do for the next few hours."

"Only gypsies read fortunes. She'll learn about us then sell our information to someone so they can rob us."

Damien rolled his eyes. "You think anyone could cross us and get away with it? Come on."

Since I didn't have a better plan of what to do next, I followed Damien inside the mysterious tent. Once the flap closed behind us, we were absorbed in dim lighting, the various lamps around the room giving off different colors.

The woman who sat at the table was covered in jewels. A blue eye was one of the largest pendants that hung down her neck. Jewels were also braided into her hair, and the rest of her brown locks were tucked underneath the shawl that tied around her chin.

The woman had an arrangement of cards in front of her, and she continued to rearrange them as if we weren't there at all.

Damien approached the table, welcoming himself into the room like he owned it. "You want to read my fortune?"

She kept working the cards, her eyes down.

Damien stared at her, slowly becoming more annoyed by her rejection.

I noticed the table in the corner where there were at least a hundred candles burning, their smells coming together to form a scent I couldn't even describe. There were small vases on the ground, gold plated with turquoise stones decorated along the sides. There were several, all the same but still unique. It was the first time I'd ever seen vases in that scheme.

Damien eventually lost his patience. "I guess you aren't getting paid today." He turned around to look at me. "Come on, let's get the hell out of here."

"Wait." The middle-aged gypsy stopped playing with her cards.

Damien grinned at me, both of his dimples showing with boyish charm. He slowly turned around, his arrogance rising like the smell from the candles. "That changed your tune quickly."

She kept the same stony face, looking at Damien without blinking once. "I was studying your auras, which are quite different. They say you don't need to speak to a man to know him. All you need to do is feel him. Now, sit." She grabbed her cards and put them into a single deck. "What's your name?"

Damien sat in the old wooden chair. "Aren't you supposed to know that?"

"No. I'm supposed to read your future. In order to do that, I need some information from you."

"My aura wasn't enough?" he asked like a smartass.

She continued to shuffle the cards as she held his gaze. "Your aura is pungent." She pushed a dish toward him. "Your payment."

"How much?" He pulled some coins out of his pocket.

"Whatever you think is fair."

Damien raised an eyebrow before tossing three coins into the jar. "Never heard that before."

The gypsy grabbed the deck of cards and then placed them on the table, organizing them into two rows. She slowly took away cards that seemed out of place until only two were left. "Give me your palm."

He rested it on the table.

She grabbed his wrist, felt around for a few seconds, and then studied the lines in his palm. "Would you like to know your future?"

"Why else would I be here?"

She continued to ignore his rough attitude, and her only response was giving him a cold look with her brown eyes. "The future is a scary thing. Knowing what will befall you is considered a curse more than a blessing."

"I'm not asking how I'm going to die. I was expecting a fortune cookie type of thing."

She raised an eyebrow. "Then maybe you should have eaten

Chinese for lunch. This is a true reading. I've had many people return to me in anger because this conversation ruined their lives."

"Right..."

I lingered in the corner, listening to their conversation as I observed the contents of the small tent. It was warm inside because there was no airflow and it was a hot summer night. But everything she had was so thick and heavy. The rugs on the floor padded the room with heat, and the fabric of the tent itself was so thick none of the outside light could penetrate through the material.

The gypsy looked into his palm once more. "Alright. You will be a rich man, Damien. Very rich."

His shoulders immediately stiffened. "Good to know."

"You will have more money than you could ever spend in one lifetime."

"Even better..."

"But you will be alone. And you will lose many people you love on the way. One woman will love you for you, not your money or your power, but you'll lose her. And once she's gone...she's gone. Your life will be filled with regret, mistakes that can never be undone."

Damn.

Damien kept his cool. "Well...at least I'll be rich." He rose from the seat and clapped me on the shoulder. "Good luck, man."

I didn't care about learning my fortune, even if it was a bunch of bullshit. But I dropped into the chair anyway. My knees were planted far apart and my hands rested in my lap because I wasn't eager for a strange woman to touch me.

The gypsy didn't look at Damien when she addressed him. "Leave us."

"What?" Damien asked. "He heard my fortune. He doesn't care if I hear his."

"Leave us," she repeated, with more resolve.

Instead of challenging her, Damien stepped out of the tent and swore under his breath.

When it was just the two of us, it became quiet, the tension slowly rising as our eyes remained locked. The sound of the surrounding crowd was still audible, but it was muffled by the thickness that insulated us.

With just her experience, she showed far more interest in me than she did with Damien. Then she took the bowl with money away.

I watched her movements then raised an eyebrow. "You won't read my fortune?"

"Yes. But I won't take your money."

That was the first time I ever heard a gypsy say that. "I don't know if I should be concerned or flattered."

"Very concerned. It's not often when someone steps inside my tent and disrupts all the energy in the room. Your presence is profound. Your future terrifies me."

This was one hell of an act. "If you think you're going to pick my pockets, not gonna happen." I had eyes in the back of my fucking head. If someone tried to stick their hand down my pants, they'd get a punch to the jaw.

She shuffled the cards then dispersed them onto the table. "I don't want your money. It's tainted."

"Tainted how?"

"Because of the way you earned it. It's blood money."

My eyes narrowed because she wasn't wrong.

She moved the cards around until she was only left with three. She examined each one. "Fire. Demon. Death."

I glanced at the cards then looked at her once more. "You picked those cards."

"No. They picked me." She grabbed my wrist and started to feel my skin. She examined my palm, a concentrated expression on her face. "All your ambitions will come true. Your blood money will make you rich, but you'll hide in plain sight. You'll pretend to be someone else and you'll fool most."

I had no idea how she knew about my money—and that concerned me.

"But your life will be a very sad story. Are you sure you want to hear it?"

If I were smart, I would just walk away now. Whether I believed her or not, she was getting into my head.

When I didn't answer, she continued. "You'll commit unforgivable crimes. You'll kill men when only the Lord should decide who lives and dies. You'll give life to those who don't deserve it and take life from others who've earned it. As punishment, you'll only love one woman for your entire life...but she'll never love you."

I couldn't picture myself loving any woman, no matter how beautiful, how sexy, or how she was between the sheets. With my riches and power, I intended to enjoy every aspect in life and every woman that would have me.

"This woman will become your wife—but she still won't love you."

I wanted to storm out and call this bullshit, but I stayed in my seat, wanting to hear the rest.

"She'll give you two sons—but still won't love you."

I couldn't picture myself being a husband or a father, but I continued to listen.

"You'll be loyal to this woman, protect her with your life, and never take another woman while she's yours—but it will never be enough. Nothing will ever be enough."

"Why would I waste my time on a woman like that?"

She examined the lines in my palm before she let me go. "Because that's the curse. You'll love this woman inexplicably. Forces outside of your control will dictate your emotions. You'll be forced to love her even if you don't want to. That will be your punishment."

"Loving someone doesn't seem like a punishment."

"Love is the most painful feeling in the world. It'll crush you, Hades. To be with the woman you love every day but know she doesn't feel the same way...that's torture."

"Then why would she marry me in the first place?"

She shrugged. "That remains to be seen." For the first time since I stepped inside that tent, she actually showed emotion—pity. She leaned back against her chair and crossed her arms over her chest, like touching me had burned her fingertips. "But the cards don't lie. You're a dangerous man...and you're only getting started."

"SERIOUSLY?" Damien asked as we walked down the pathway to the brothel on the other side of the bazaar. "You're not going to tell me what she said?"

"It was bullshit anyway."

"Then all the more reason."

"She's just some poor gypsy wanting to take our cash. I'm sure she tried to pick-pocket us a few times."

"Didn't look like it to me." He continued to look at me as he walked by my side. "So what? You're just never going to tell me?"

"If it's bullshit anyway, what does it matter?"

He shrugged. "Maybe it's not bullshit. You never know. She didn't know my name, so she can't be that good."

My feet stopped moving and halted in my tracks.

Damien took a few more steps before he realized I'd fallen behind. He turned around and looked at me. "What?"

She knew my name.

Damien hadn't said it all day. There was no way she overheard. My license didn't even show that name.

Damien raised an eyebrow. "Everything okay, man?"

I moved forward again, going through the motions even though I was still shocked. "Yeah...I'm fine."

CHAPTER One

Sofia

It was one of those big parties, the kind where so many people are invited that you're only going to know a handful of people there. Publicity was important to my parents. As one of the most famous hotel owners in the country, my father had an image to uphold. Success. Popularity. Money. Those were all important to him.

But mostly important to my mother.

It was the grand opening of our new hotel in Florence, Tuscan Rose. With three hundred rooms, a gorgeous lobby, three pools, and everything anyone would want for a summer vacation in Italy.

I was only eighteen years old, but someday, this hotel would be mine. I would run it with the same integrity my father did, with the same attention to detail, and the best customer service any guest could ask for.

But for tonight, I was still too young to even think about those things. In my black party dress with my hair pulled to one side, I stepped into the ball room and watched everyone mingle, holding cocktails as they appreciated the chandeliers hanging from the ceiling, the wagyu appetizers being handed out by the waiters.

I stood off to the side and stared at them all. It was a fun party, but since I was the youngest person there, I felt out of place.

My father came out of the crowd, tall, lean, and with a moustache that had been there since I could remember and placed his hand at the small of my back. "There you are, Sofia. I wanted to introduce you to a couple of people."

I was tired of meeting new people that I would never remember. Their faces wouldn't register, and their names would only be in my brain for two seconds before I forgot those too. I was proud of my father and everything he accomplished, but I was also bored by the whole ordeal. "Sure."

He guided me to a group of older men. We shook hands, exchanged pleasantries, and my father proudly introduced me as his beautiful daughter. More pleasantries were exchanged before they moved away.

Then the most beautiful man in the world walked right up to us. Young, muscular, and with a shadow on his jawline the way I liked, he confidently approached us both and shook my father's hand.

"Congratulations, Peter. This hotel will be here for hundreds of years." He held himself perfectly straight, a handsome face on a strong frame. His black suit was nearly the color of his dark hair, and his brown eyes looked like two pieces of melted chocolate. He was definitely older than me, but much younger than the rest of the guests at the party.

When he shifted his gaze to me, my knees grew weak, and I felt so damn shy. I was usually mouthy and sassy, but all that attitude disappeared when I came face to face with a real man.

He was nothing like the boys I'd liked before.

He was mature..like wine or aged beef.

I shouldn't have looked at him that way. He was too old for me.

The man shifted his gaze to me then extended his hand. "You must be Sofia. Your father has told me so much about you."

It took a few seconds for me to react, to reciprocate his gesture with a handshake.

He squeezed my hand firmly and then let go.

"It's nice to meet you too," I forced myself to say.

His eyes lingered on mine for a moment longer before he turned back to my father. "Lovely party. I expect we'll be here all night."

"I hope so. I paid for a lot of booze, so we better drink it all." He chuckled then looked at me. "This fine young man is making a name for himself in the finance world. I suspect he'll be a big asset to us in a few years."

"Yes," he said. "You're probably right." He politely excused himself. "Have a good evening, Mr. Romano."

"You too." When he was gone, my father turned back to me. "Having a good time, Sofia?"

I'd been pretty bored...until that man showed up. "Yeah...I think I am."

***

I TRIED NOT to make my stare obvious, but it seemed like every time I looked at that hot man, he was already looking at me.

So he caught my stare.

I combated the redness in my cheeks as much as possible, but no amount of foundation could keep the color at bay. My eyes drifted to a table where a pack of cigarettes lay, an unguarded lighter was there as well. Even though there were so many people in the room, it made it easy to sneak around and get away with anything. I grabbed a cigarette, lit it, and then walked outside.

It was late so the balcony was deserted. The distant sound of voices carried through the windows and thudded against my eardrum. Every bit of laughter was obnoxious because it was so fake.

That was why I hated these events.

Publicity stunts.

I leaned against the wall, out of sight, and enjoyed my cigarette with my arms crossed and one foot planted against the wall.

From the top story of the hotel, I had a prime view of Florence, the lights brilliant and beautiful. A breeze was in the air and it licked the sweat that formed on the back of my neck. Being separated from the herd was nice because I wouldn't be tempted to stare at that sexy man.

The sexy man that was way out of my league.

I continued to pull the smoke into my lungs and let it drift from my nostrils. My parents had no idea I smoked, but they were aware I loved wine more than they did. With every drag of nicotine, I became calm, tapping my finger against the tip so the ashes would fall to the floor.

My wrist relaxed as my head rested against the wall, feeling the fatigue settle in my veins when I realized it must be one in the morning by now. The crowd continued to party but it couldn't last much longer.

I only closed my eyes for a few seconds when the cigarette was ripped from my fingers.

Shit. I'd been caught.

My eyes opened and settled on the man that had stolen my attention since the moment I lay eyes on him.

He brought the cigarette to his lips, took a deep drag, and let the smoke drift away with the breeze. "You don't strike me as a smoker."

My heart raced a million miles in my chest, and I lost all my confidence in the blink of an eye. This man made me so nervous I could barely breathe, let alone think of a comeback. "Occasionally."

"Occasionally is just as bad as regularly."

"I don't see why."

"Either one takes years off your life." He took another drag off my cigarette then looked over the edge of the balcony to the city below. The smoke lifted from his lips, and he looked so sexy standing there.

"Maybe you should take your own advice."

He shrugged. "I don't plan to live long."

I extended my palm. "Can I have it back?" Even if it was just to feel the moisture of his mouth against the tip of that cigarette. It was like a dirty kiss, nicotine and smoke mixed in between.

"No." He crushed it within his palm without wincing then threw it in the garbage can.

"That was rude."

"I'm an asshole, so no surprise there." He stood with his body perpendicular to mine and stared at the marvelous view from our fancy party. His hands slid into the pockets of his suit as he enjoyed the fresh air with me.

I did my best to play it cool. "Are you going to tell my father?"

"I'm not a rat." He slowly turned his gaze back to me, his brown eyes innately pretty. He seemed too handsome to be true, like Prince Charming in a fairy-tale. He'd been a lot nicer inside, but now he seemed moody, off-putting. But he continued to linger there anyway...like he wanted to be with me.

"Thanks. But you could have given me back that cigarette."

"Trust me, I'm looking out for you." He stepped closer to me, bringing us close together so we could drop our voices further. If someone came outside, they would see us in deep conversation and probably assume something inappropriate was happening. But no one was going to come out at that time of night, at least I hoped not.

I'd dated guys while in school, but I never had a serious boyfriend. Now that I was officially an adult who was about to start business school at the university, I expected that to change.

Maybe it would change tonight.

"I don't need someone to look out for me." I kept my arms crossed over my chest and leaned against the wall, feigning indifference. But something told me this man could see right through that. "How do you know my father?"

"We do business together." He didn't elaborate further. Maybe he thought his job was boring and didn't want to drone on about it.

That was unfortunate because I genuinely wanted to know. "One day, I'm going to take over for my father and run this hotel."

"Ambitious…I like that."

I tried to hide my smile, but the corner of my lip raised slightly.

"Nothing sexier than a woman knowing what she wants." His voice was deep like dark chocolate. It rumbled deep in his throat before it emerged, sweet on the ears. This man looked beautiful, sounded beautiful…he just was beautiful.

"Do you know what you want?"

He turned his gaze toward me, his jawline hard like it was chiseled from stone. "Yes. I take ambition a little too far."

Bumps appeared on my arms even though it was still humid and warm. My nipples pressed against my bra and I resisted the urge to fidget. This was the first man who made me feel passion and lust, like the kind they showed in books and movies. The other boys I'd been interested in were practically friends. This guy was…a man. "I never got your name."

He slowly turned back to the balcony. "Hades."

I couldn't control the eyebrow that rose up my face. "That's your name?"

"Yes. Not as beautiful as Sofia, but it will do."

"Isn't that the god of the underworld?"

"Yes, to those who believe in Greek mythology. Are you one of those people?"

"No. But it's still an interesting name."

He was standoffish and cold, staring at the view of the city that was practically laid at our feet. Even with his hands in his pockets, he stood perfectly straight, having a strong back and an ass that looked great in those slacks. "It's a name you don't forget easily." He turned away and headed back to the doorway without saying goodbye.

I didn't want him to go. He was the first interesting person I met at the party, and I wasn't eager to lose my only friend...and whatever else I wanted him to be. "Going to steal more cigarettes?"

He stopped and slowly turned, slight amusement in his eyes. He came back toward me, taking his time because he knew I wasn't going anywhere. "Taking cigarettes isn't exactly a hobby."

"Fooled me. So will I see you around?"

His eyes shifted back and forth slightly as they looked into mine. "Do you want to see me around, Sofia?"

The way he said my name made chills run down my spine. Boys would make up a lie and walk away, but this was a man who got right to the point. He wasn't afraid to confront me, to make me uncomfortable with that deep stare.

I wanted to respond with some smartass comment, but I didn't want to play games. This man wasn't playing games with me, so why should I play games with him? "Yes."

A slight look of surprise came into his gaze at my honesty. His lips slightly pressed together as he continued to look at me, as if some internal argument made him clench his entire body. His eyes were open, and he hardly blinked as he stared at me. "You're a beautiful girl, Sofia. One day, you're going to be a gorgeous woman. Maybe then you'll see me around." He gently put me down, but it still hurt.

I didn't expect anything from him, but knowing he would walk away and I would probably never see him again was a huge disappointment. The first man I actually felt some heat for was out of my league. "How old are you?"

He grinned slightly, showing his natural charm. "Too old."

I hadn't lifted my body from the wall. So far, I'd managed to get him to stay with just my words. But eventually, he would walk away and words wouldn't be enough to keep him close. "And how old is too old?"

He came closer to me, his shoulder making contact with the wall. His voice lowered to a whisper. "Twenty-five."

That meant he was seven years older than me. He had seven more years of experience, seven more years of women in his bed.

And I hadn't taken anyone to bed.

He watched my reaction. "Like I said, too old." He turned away, dismissing our conversation for good.

I would leave for university in Milan for a few months, so I suspected I would never see this man again. I was a new adult that was flooded with hormones and I wanted a real kiss, a real experience that would make me feel like a woman. This man was the first one that turned me on, that made me want to take off my clothes and lose my virginity. But he wouldn't be around for that.

So I grabbed him by the arm and pulled him into me. Knowing this could never be more, that this could never be anything but a secret, I put myself on the line and dug my fingers into his hair as I kissed him.

Instead of pulling away, he kissed me back. He smiled against my mouth slightly as he pressed me further into the wall, his hard body so strong against my softness. "Alright, baby. Just one." His hand slid into the back of my hair and he craned my head down so he could kiss me hard. His warm breath filled my mouth and the hard outline of his dick pressed right into my stomach. He gave me his tongue, gave me his passion.

I took it all. My hands snaked up his back and I held him close to me, wanting to feel something real instead of the stagnant fakeness my family exuded. I didn't have the perfect family like everyone believed. My parents didn't love each other. Sometimes I wasn't sure if they even loved me.

But this was real.

It was wrong, so wrong that Hades could be shot if he got caught pressed up against me, but he kissed me like he didn't have a care in the world. With his back turned to everything else but us, he grabbed my thigh and wrapped it around his torso, thrusting his package into the perfect spot between my legs.

Oh yes...

He stopped our kiss so he could watch my reaction, see the way I responded to the friction.

I liked it...a lot. "Ooh..."

His hand remained fisted in my hair. "Has a man ever made you come, baby?"

I was so embarrassed that I wanted to lie, but when I looked into those brown eyes, I wanted to say nothing but the truth. "No..."

His lips moved to mine again and he kissed me slowly, grinding up against me in the nighttime air. I could feel the wetness in my panties, and he could probably feel them against his slacks at this point. Every kiss was dynamite. Every kiss was fire. I'd never been kissed so good, never had my toes curl so hard. Was this what it always felt like? Was this the kind of heat every couple felt?

He grinded harder and harder, my dress sliding up as he rubbed into me. He sucked my bottom lip into his mouth then gave me another thrust.

A thrust that made me so white-hot that I thought someone set me on fire. Whimpers escaped my lips, and I wanted to scream until my lungs gave out.

He kept his mouth over mine and muffled the noise, letting me finish my climax without fear.

It was so good.

Euphoric.

God, I wanted to do that again.

He kissed me a few more times before he pulled away, slightly out of breath with tousled hair. He kept his face close to mine, his deep breathing quiet. "You're a virgin." He didn't phrase it as a question, like he already knew the answer without asking.

I didn't correct him.

"Can I give you some advice?"

I gave a slight nod.

"In a few years, every man in the world is going to chase you. But most men are assholes. Most men will treat you like garbage and throw you away. Don't let them. Don't waste your time on someone that doesn't deserve you. You're a beautiful woman with a powerful surname. Don't be one of those girls that lets losers fuck her. Be that woman that only lets a king fuck her."

"Are you a king?" I blurted, my words coming out as a whisper.

His eyes shifted back and forth slightly as he held my gaze. "I'm the king."

***

CHAPTER TWO

Four Years Later

Sofia

I lifted my suitcase onto my old bed then opened the top. Stacks of jeans, tops, and dresses were inside, all the things I wore while I was at university in Milan. For four years, I studied business and poetry. I learned everything I possibly could about running a business, operating an ethical company that treated it employees with dignity, and how to keep the business open for decades.

My family owned a line of hotels throughout Italy, ranging from the boot in the south all the way to the north close to Nice, France. As the only child of my parents, I was the heir to take over the family business.

I intended to make our hotels outlive our family by many generations. I was most acquainted with the hotel in Milan since I'd been studying there for the last four years, but the hotel in Florence was my favorite. I witnessed my father build it from the ground up, making his dream into a reality with such calm suaveness. I never told him how proud I was of his work, and now that he was dead, I regretted it every single day of my life.

Now I was back in Florence, moving back in with my mother until I found my own footing. Living alone for the last few years gave me a taste of independence that I didn't want to relinquish. I lived in a small apartment, but I had the freedom to eat cereal before bed, have men spend the night, and let my laundry pile up until it was a behemoth on the floor in the corner of my room. My booze and cigarettes could be enjoyed without a judgmental gaze.

My mother lived with my stepfather in the same mansion I grew up in, three stories right in the heart of the city. It wasn't like we wouldn't have the privacy we needed from one another.

But still, a grown woman shouldn't be living with her mother.

I finished unpacking then went to the terrace on the second floor, where we had breakfast every morning in the summer before it got too hot. It was almost fall, so the temperature was somewhat diminishing. The humidity was taking a little longer.

Mother sat there, her legs crossed with a cigarette resting between her soft fingertips. She had a dark brown hair just like mine, perfectly manicured to maintain her beauty. She still had beautiful skin, her wrinkles hidden under all the products she used to fight the detrimental effects of aging.

With my eyebrow raised, I approached her from behind and snatched the cigarette from her poised hand. "Things have changed around here."

She maintained her calm posture, her eyes following my movements as I took a seat. A cup of coffee was on the table beside her, just black even though she preferred cream and sugar. "Not really. I just don't bother to hide it anymore."

"Smoking takes years off your life." Anytime I felt a cigarette between my fingertips, I thought of the erotic night I had on a balcony four years ago. A man took it right out of my hand and tossed it away.

"I don't care." She opened the pack and pulled out another.

"It causes wrinkles..."

She had the cigarette in her mouth with the lighter held close to the tip. Instead of striking it with her thumb and making it burst into flame, she sighed and put everything down.

"That's what I thought." That was the kind of woman my mother was. She cared more about her appearance than living a long, healthy life.

"Don't be so prissy. I've found your stash around the house."

I didn't deny it. They say mothers know everything. They were right.

A servant brought me a cup of coffee, but I didn't hesitate before I added cream and sugar. I liked it fattening, packed with sugar and calories, and I didn't give a damn about the destruction to my waistline. "I quit a few years ago."

"Why?"

"Because I want to live past forty."

"Now that's an exaggeration." Instead of reaching for her cigarettes, she grabbed her coffee and took a sip. She examined the city before us, the sun rising over the beautiful city, highlighting the green hillsides in the background. Even from miles away, the scent of grapes was always in the air. "How does it feel to be home?"

"It's nice..."

She chuckled. "You hate it, don't you?"

"I'm just not thrilled to be moving back in with my mother."

"I lived with my parents until I got married."

"But you got married when you were nineteen."

She shrugged. "There's nothing to be ashamed of. Soon enough, the same will happen to you."

I didn't have any interest in getting married. I loved my parents, but their marriage was depressing. My mother's second marriage to my stepfather was even worse. My mother only gave herself to a man for one reason—to be taken care of. She wanted a man to handle the business, the finances, and be the alpha in the relationship.

That sounded like mindless slavery to me.

I had much bigger ambitions in life. "I'm going to work with Gustavo tomorrow. He's gonna show me a few things about the hotel, give me a job so I can learn as much as possible." It never made sense to me that my mother remarried and handed the title to her business to her new husband. That just seemed stupid to me.

She slowly turned to me, not even bothering to cover the disdain from her eyes. "Honey, men are supposed to work. Women make other people work for them."

"It's not just a random job. I want to take over the hotel business when Gustavo retires."

"Your husband can handle that."

I loved my mother, but her ancient outlook on marriage was so archaic that she seemed senile. "Maybe that was true a hundred years ago, but things have changed. I'm perfectly capable of handling our company on my own."

"I know you're a bright girl with a lot of brilliant ideas. But it doesn't matter how smart you are. It doesn't mean you can get things done."

My fingers rested on the top of my coffee, the heat reaching my skin. Even simple conversations with my mother turned into wars across the battlefield. She was so stubborn and opinionated that even mundane conversations were unbearable. "What's that supposed to mean?"

"It means..." She took a sip of her coffee then set it down beside her. "That no matter how hard you try, people will never respect you the way they would respect a man. They won't listen to you or value your ideas. Anytime you give delegations, they'll assume you're being an overbearing bitch. People will push you around and take advantage of you. That's just the world we live in...which is why you need a powerful husband that can protect your wealth and interests."

It was such a load of horseshit. "If you really believe that, why did you encourage me to attend university?"

"To get your M.R.S. Degree."

"Excuse me?" I asked, an eyebrow raised.

"I wanted you to meet a good man and settle down. But you came back without a ring on your finger."

"I wasn't shopping for a husband. I was only interested in learning."

She shrugged then kept looking at the breathtaking view, the sight that only we got to witness. Most people would never know the wealth we got to enjoy—and we didn't even work for it. "You're still young so enjoy yourself, Sofia. Date the men you'll never marry. Screw the guys that will only hold your interest for a night. Because eventually...all that fun stuff ends. That's one of my regrets...not enjoying my youth. I immediately married your father...wish I'd let loose first."

I'd definitely been letting loose, and the casual detachment was simple. Maybe if I met a man I really liked, things would be different. But the idea of settling down into boring mediocrity sounded terrible. I wanted to be an executive, I wanted to have flings, and I wanted to have a family someday...even if I did it on my own. But being tied down to one man forever...sounded terrible. "I'm only twenty-two. I have a lot of youth left inside me."

"Then enjoy it. But don't get your hopes up about running that hotel."

The sexism surprised me, especially coming from my own mother. "It's nice to be home…"

She chuckled, picking up on my sarcasm. "I can't wait for you to move out either."

GUSTAVO MARRIED my mother just three months after my father was gone.

He was a widower, having lost his wife in a terrible car accident just a few years before my father died. He had one son, who lived out of the house and already started his own family. I didn't know the specifics of their nuptials, but I knew it was negotiated like a contract.

But in any case, I liked him.

He was kind, affectionate, and treated my mom well. When I saw them together, they seemed like friends more than man and wife. Maybe that was why their relationship worked so well. My mother wanted a man to take care of her, and Gustavo didn't want to be lonely.

It could be worse, so I let it be.

We went to the Tuscan Rose together and entered the lobby. Several chandeliers hung from the ceiling, the crystals on fire as the light shined through the prisms. White vases with fresh flowers lined the tables and dressers, and mirrors on the wall showed how expansive the room really was. I loved the energy the second I stepped inside, loved the excitement of the customers as they checked in at the front desk. It was impeccably clean, a visual representation of the Romano family name.

"I suggest you start with a concierge position." Instead of leading me to the back where the offices were located, he stopped in the lobby. "You know so much about this city, and you're so good with people. It's a great start."

I looked up at him in surprise, finding no comfort in the warm look he gave me. He was a tall man, taller than my father had been, and his dark skin showed his exotic origins. He wore eyeglasses on the bridge of his nose. In conversation, he was a polite and restrained man, but when his eyes lit up in warmth, he was a whole new person. "I'm not interested in the concierge position. I was hoping to shadow you, to look at the bookkeeping and do whatever other managerial positions I can assist with."

He smile never faded. "I realize that, but—"

"Don't listen to my mother. I know how she feels about this, but this is my legacy, and I intend to hold on to it." I wouldn't get married just to have another man control my company. I didn't need anyone's assistance but my own.

His smile slowly faded. "This is her hotel, Sofia. I don't have a lot of say in the matter."

"You obviously do if you're running it." I stood my ground and refused to back down. I would only get what I wanted in life if I fought for it. It didn't make sense that my mother's second husband got to manage what belonged to our family. It should either be my mother or me.

He sighed as he lowered his gaze. "I was under the impression you needed money."

"Yes. I've got to move out as quickly as possible."

He chuckled. "I can imagine. But I can't offer you a position as a manager or anything of that nature. You have excellent marks at university, but experience is more important in an occupation like this. You'll have to start at the bottom."

"I never said I had a problem with that." I didn't expect to be given everything just because of my last name, but I did expect the chance to prove my worthiness. "I'll take the concierge position if you teach me everything about running this hotel. I can work with you in the morning and do the concierge position in the evenings."

"You mean business, don't you?"

"Always." I placed one hand on my hip, looking up at my stepfather without moving an inch. I refused to let this go without at least fighting for it. Maybe the concierge job would pay enough to cover my rent, and with enough time, I would prove to my stepfather and mother that I was capable of taking over when the time was right.

Gustavo was the man in the relationship, but he possessed much more compassion than she ever did. He didn't seem to possess the same sexist viewpoint that she did. "Alright. Let's keep this between us—for now."

I moved into his chest and hugged him. "Thank you, Gustavo. It means so much to me."

***

Gustavo had an office and a conference room off to the side of the hotel. There were several other offices, belonging to personnel involved with daily operations of the hotel. One office was empty and a title wasn't listed on the door.

I worked with Gustavo for the day, shadowing his movements and understanding the duties of a manager of the hotel. Technically, he had a general manager that oversaw the employees, but he was responsible for the financial aspect. I got to see the book-keeping sheets, seeing how much money the hotel earned on a daily basis. It was impressive—especially during the off season.

The hours passed quickly, and I couldn't help but assume my

mother was an idiot. Man or woman, it didn't matter. Anyone could run this hotel if they were passionate about it. I wanted to tell my mother to return to ancient times, because the present didn't suit her well.

Gustavo printed off a few spreadsheets then laid them across the desk. "I have a meeting in just a few minutes. How about you focus on this until I'm finished?"

"What's the meeting about?"

"Money," he said, half joking. "Everything is always about money." He was just to step outside when a man appeared in the doorway. Tall, muscular, and wearing a suit like a second skin, he wasn't the kind of guest I expected...because he was so young.

I was sitting at the desk, my eyes taking in the man in the gray suit. With brown eyes that seemed both dangerous and warm, he had a familiar face. With high cheekbones and a masculine tightness to his features, his appearance immediately ran a bell. It'd been so many years since I'd last seen him that I almost didn't recognize him.

He'd been a man the last time I saw him. But now...he was a bigger man.

With broad shoulders and tight forearms, his masculine characteristics were noticeable through his clothes. A shiny watch was on his rich, an Omega, probably worth tens of thousands of euros. His thumb casually brushed over his bottom lip as he entered, his chin covered with a thick shadow that hadn't been shaved in days. The chords in his neck were distinct, especially since his skin was tan and tight. He had full lips, perfect for a hot kiss in the darkness of a cold bedroom. Those eyes were so powerful that could make a woman spread her knees in just seconds.

I had some decent lovers in Milan...but none of them looked like this man.

Hades.

He addressed my stepfather first. "Gustavo."

My stepfather walked to him and shook his hand. "Thanks for coming by. I know you're a busy man."

"A man is never too busy to make money." It was the first time his eyes turned to me, and without giving any significant reaction, it was clear that he recognized me. It was the subtle narrowing of his eyes, the slight clench of his hard jaw. Slowly, his hands returned to his pockets as he studied me.

When we first met, I was nothing but a shy girl. I was barely an adult and didn't possess the courage to handle an experienced man. His confidence unnerved me, made me back up against the wall and turn rigid in fear.

But not anymore.

I rose to my feet and glided to him, working my heels like they were comfortable sandals. With my hand outstretched, I greeted him like he was a business associate. "Nice to see you again, Hades."

He didn't pull his hand out of his pocket for a second, as if my offer was inappropriate. Our first meeting had been anything but professional. We were two walking hormones that grinded up against the wall like it was our last night on earth. I still thought about that climax sometimes, the first one of its kind. It was powerful, profound, and so much better than the pathetic ones the boys had given me.

He finally took my hand. His fingers moved all the way to my wrist, and he immediately squeezed me with tension, the pressure making my blood circulate in both fear and arousal. His eyes never left mine, and he didn't seem to care if my stepfather picked up on the heat between us. "I'm sorry about your father. He was a good man." It didn't feel like a false sentiment. My father had been dead for years and he didn't need to acknowledge it. Seemed like he meant it.

I dropped the handshake first. "Thank you."

"Good, you're acquainted." Gustavo gave me a gentle pat on the back before he stepped out of the door and into the hallway. "Hades and I will take an hour, maybe more."

"Can I sit in?" I asked, knowing he would say no.

"Not today," Gustavo said. "In time." He rounded the corner.

Hades lingered for a second longer, letting his eyes take me in like he could easily picture me naked. An innate confidence burned in his eyes, like nothing and no one could ever make him question who he was. He took a gentle step back, not wanting to take his eyes off me. Then he finally turned around.

My eyes immediately went to his ass.

Still tight, I see.

CHAPTER Three

Sofia

I didn't see Hades again.

I wasn't entirely sure what business he had with Gustavo. He mentioned something about working in finance a long time ago, but I couldn't recall the specifics. Maybe he never even told me that information...I just assumed. When I asked Gustavo all he said was, "He handles the money."

That didn't make sense.

I was determined to be a respectable member of the team at Tuscan Rose so I wouldn't get involved with someone that was also on the payroll, not that I assumed anything would happen in the first place. That kiss happened four years ago and we were complete strangers. Perhaps he was just as bored at that party as I was, so he followed me outside just to get away from the stiffness.

I could feel embarrassed by our past, but I refused. It was one moment, one night. Nothing much to say about it. He was even sexier than I remembered so I couldn't pretend that he wasn't a walking piece of eye candy. He was gorgeous...plain and simply. But gorgeous men were only good for one thing.

Fucking.

I started my shift in the concierge department that night, helping American guests decide where to make dinner reservations in this historic town. Most of them were newlyweds, so their excitement was palpable. I also booked a few spa treatments, and by nine, I finally got to walk out the door.

Instead of heading home...to my mother's...I decided to go out instead. I had a few friends in Florence and after a few texts we met somewhere crowded and dark, going straight for the hard liquor and skipping the wine.

I had wine for breakfast. That was practically water to me at this point.

"How's the new job?" Esme had blonde hair and blue eyes, looking nothing like me but definitely more beautiful. She wore a white dress with a black blazer on top, finished with her job at the art gallery.

"It's gonna pay my bills so it's pretty good."

She chuckled. "Are you in training to take over?"

"Yes and no. Right now I'm just shadowing my stepfather and doing a few small tasks."

"Not a bad way to get paid." She had a scotch—neat. Her nails were painted fiery red, which was an interesting color against her fair skin.

"I actually don't get paid for that. That's all volunteer."

"Then how do you plan to pay your bills...?" She cocked an eyebrow as she took a drink. "You got a sugar daddy?"

"No. I work the concierge gig in the evenings."

"Ooh...not nearly as exciting as having a sugar daddy."

I chuckled. "No. Not even close."

"What's it like so far? Do you help a lot of hot businessmen taking their mistresses to their rooms?"

"No. I'm sure they would be more secretive than to stop by for a chat. They don't care about eating the best pasta or visiting the Barsetti winery for wine tasting. All they care about is fucking and getting room service."

"Oooh..." A dreamy look came into her eyes. "Sex and room service. That sounds like a dream."

"It does..." It'd been a while since I had good man between the sheets. My lovers were casual, nothing serious because I never intended to stay in Milan for more than a couple of years. Being a student was a good way to meet new people, especially men my own age. But I never had a deeply passionate relationship, the kind where you couldn't keep your hands off each other for more than a few minutes. Maybe that was love. Or maybe that was combustive lust.

"Are you seeing anyone?"

"Me?" I asked incredulously. "No. Not while I'm still living with my mother."

"How's that going?"

"It's not terrible. I mean, we have so much space it's not like we're fighting to use the bathroom or the laundry machine. It's just weird to live under her roof again, like I'm a child or a failed adult. I miss bringing men home. Now I can't do that anymore."

"I'm sure you could sneak him in."

"Eh...don't really want to do that." That would make me seem dishonest and childish.

"Couldn't you just stay at his place?"

"I suppose. But then my mother will wonder where I've been all night..."

"No, she'll know where you've been all night," she said with a smile. "You're a grown woman so I doubt she'll give you a hard time about it."

"Yeah..." My mother was a very blunt person and she even encouraged me to enjoy my youth as much as possible, be with all the men that would never be my husband, get it out of my system before I settled down with a suitable partner. "She probably wouldn't care. Probably wouldn't ask me any questions. But I guess it's just awkward giving her an idea of what I'm doing in my private life."

"I always thought the two of you were close." Esme was incredulous to all the attention she was capturing. Lots of men behind her wouldn't stop staring at her, probably deciding if they should buy her a drink or just walk up and talk to her.

"We are. I love my mother. We just don't see eye to eye on a lot of things. When my father passed away, we became a lot closer." My parents were never in love, but it was obvious my mother's sadness at his passing was genuine. She lost a friend...a partner.

One of the men that had his eyes on her finally made his move. Tall and handsome, he had a nice smile and shoulders built for strength. He appeared on her right side, his hands in his pockets so he wouldn't seem overly eager. "Hello, I'm Kyle." He extended his hand to shake hers.

When her eyes widened in approval, I knew she liked what she saw. "Esme." She shook his hand. "This is my friend Sofia."

He shook my hand. "Lovely to meet you both."

They became engaged in conversation, making each other laugh and exchanging subtle cues of affection.

I silently excused myself so my friend could get laid. I brought my drink to another table and took a seat. Sitting alone anywhere besides the bar was awkward but I wasn't ready to go home just yet. I wanted to enjoy this last bit of vodka cranberry before I walked home.

My eyes wandered around the bar, people-watching. There were a few packs of women at the bar, gathered close together and chatting over a bottle of wine. A lot of the men were looking in their direction.

But some were looking at me.

I didn't see anyone I was interested in so I kept my gaze averted.

My eyes scanned to the left, and it stopped immediately when I noticed a man I recognized. Sitting in a dark booth facing the rest of the bar, he wore a white color shirt with black slacks and dress shoes. With his jacket missing, the hardness of his body was unmistakable. His pecs were easily to visualize, and he such strong shoulders that they stretched the fabric of his shirt and made it tight. His tan skin contrasted against the white fabric of his shirt, making him look worshipped by the sun. His head was slightly turned toward the woman beside him, the brunette that squeezed his thigh under the table and whispered into his ear.

Her blue eyes were glued to his side profile, her eyes heavy with lust and affection. She looked at that man like he was all she wanted in this world, that she wanted to take him home and never let him leave. Her hand grazed right over his crotch then slowly moved up his chest, pampering him as she slid toward his neck.

Hades had his arm around her shoulders but didn't shower her in the same affection. He looked at her indirectly and allowed her to touch him, to let her claim him as hers. She was a beautiful woman that a man would give up anything to be with, but to him, she didn't seem that important.

She moved her body into him, pressing her tits against his arm and chest as she whispered something into his ear.

He grinned when he heard whatever dirty thing she just said.

I hardly knew Hades so I couldn't make assumptions about his character, but from what I was watching, he was like every other handsome and successful man. He was in the game indefinitely, never retiring his jersey. She was just another notch on his bedpost.

But to her, she thought she won the jackpot.

I'd been a victim of that handsome grin, of those pretty eyes that made you melt. I'd only spoken to him for minutes when I dug my fingers into his hair and yanked him against me. He oozed masculinity, and he reeked of good sex. I told myself I was a young girl giving into my hormones, but I still felt the same level of attraction toward him now. He was a safe bet, a man that wouldn't take you home then let you down.

I continued to enjoy my drink and watch them, wishing I were going home with a hunk myself. It was nice to wash off the workday with a glass of booze, but getting fucked by a big dick was better.

Hades eventually turned away from her and looked ahead, probably intending to order another drink since his was empty. It only took him a second to notice me sitting alone in the booth with the black leather. His jaw didn't tighten and his eyes didn't narrow in recognition. He had no reaction at all—a perfect poker face.

Once our eyes had locked for several seconds, I turned away and kept nursing my drink. When the waitress came by, I would close my tab and head home. Esme was gonna stay with a handsome guy, and the last man I had an erotic encounter with in Florence was just feet away from me, a woman about to give him a hand job under the table. I should just call it quits and head home.

From the corner of my eye, I saw Hades have a brief conversation with his date then slide out of the booth. When he stood, the air in the room changed, a spark had been ignited. He moved down the stairs and came toward me.

I took a long drink of my glass and ignored him.

He invited himself into the leather booth, sliding in until he was close beside me.

I couldn't help but take a peek at the woman he'd been with just seconds ago. She watched him turn his attention on me with fire in her gaze. She looked equally enraged and equally hurt.

He sat beside me, his body pivoted toward me with one arm on the table. His silver watch was visible just underneath the sleeve of his collared shirt. He smelled like sandalwood and smoke, like he was a man that spent his time outdoors in the forest. Silence passed between us, the music over the speakers not loud enough to fill the void in conversation.

I refused to speak first, so I continued to drink like he wasn't there.

Hades wasn't unnerved by my indifference. He continued to stare at me, comfortable with the unspoken feud raging between us. His brown eyes watched my movements, watched me sip my glass then return it to the table. Every movement I made went noticed.

Now I started to get uncomfortable, started to break under that formidable stare. But I refuse to give any indication that I was tense, that I was the same shy girl that he met four years ago.

To break the ice, I pushed my glass toward him.

He lifted the glass, stirred the ice, and then took a drink. He set it down and slid it back toward me. "Piss."

"Better than what you're drinking."

"I'm not drinking anything."

I held up my glass. "Exactly." I took another drink and watched Esme get lost in her conversation with her new friend. She didn't seem to notice that I disappeared. She was probably so smitten with the guy that everything else ceased to matter.

The corner of his mouth rose in a smile, just slightly. Then he subtly raised his hand and immediately got the attention of the waiter. Without looking at him, he ordered. "Scotch, neat, double."

The waiter ran off, fetched the drink, and then set it on the table.

Hades slid it toward me then gave a slight nod.

Just to prove a point, I took a drink without making a sour face, and then slid it back to him. "Piss."

This time, both corners of his mouth rose in a smile.

I drank from my glass a little more often than usual, feeling the nerves get to me. I assumed he would say a couple of words then return to his date, but he continued to linger like his agenda hadn't been fulfilled.

"My assumption was incorrect." He stirred his glass and took another drink. "You are far more beautiful than I ever could have predicted." This man was confident enough to speak his mind without fear of the consequences, to tell a woman she was beautiful without being timid of her response. The sting of rejection had never pierced his skin, so he didn't carry scars like the rest of us.

I shouldn't be flattered by that comment, but in all honesty, I was. "Am I still too young for you?" I could still smell the nighttime air on my nose, feel the bumps on my arms, the taste of smoke in my mouth. It was a lifetime ago, when I was a completely different person, but it all came rushing back to me. At the time our age difference didn't matter. He was a gorgeous man that I wanted to sink my claws into. I assumed I was an adult that could handle anything. But now that I was older, I knew he made the right call when he walked away. He gave into a moment of weakness and kissed me, but he didn't let it grow into something else. He really was too old for me...we both knew it.

He set his glass down and let his lightly colored eyes look into mine, pierce my gaze like he could see everything underneath my skin. He could see my heartbeat, see my damaged soul. He could see the curves of my body through my tight dress, notice the sharpness of my tits. He slowly brought his hand to his mouth and dragged his fingers across his lips, as if he was catching a drop of scotch that somehow missed his tongue. He was clearly uncomfortable in the tense silence between words. It was like he fed off the heat. "Definitely not." His eyes slightly lowered, giving me a quick glance over before he lifted his eyes to meet my look again. One hand grasped his glass while the other stayed on his thigh.

The lock between our gazes started to make me sweat. He was better at this game than I was, so I took a drink to wash away the tension in the chords of my neck. All my muscles tightened painfully, making me rigid. I vowed I would never let a man affected my confidence, but Hades was an opponent I could never beat.

"Following in your father's footsteps?"

"Trying to."

"Still ambitious, I see." He glanced around the bar, his eyes gently scanning his surroundings for nothing in particular. "That's sexy in a woman."

"Sexy in a man too."

He turned back to me. "Then you won't be able to keep your hands off me."

"I'm doing it right now."

He grinned slightly. "Give it time."

I wanted to destroy his confidence, but I couldn't because he was right. Just like every other woman in the world, this man had me. He already watched me yank him into my arms and kiss him while my family could catch us at any moment. My cards were already on the table.

"Take my advice?" He rubbed his thumb against his glass, wiping away the condensation.

"About getting fucked?" I asked bluntly.

He gave a slight nod.

"That's a personal question and it's none of your business."

"It is my business." He turned to me, freezing in my place with that serious look. His brown eyes were beautiful in that masculine face, his dark hair around his jaw, the beautiful structure of his countenance...everything made him perfect. "Because I'm going to fuck you."

The second he said the last word, my heart spiked and started to pulse like I was about to sprint a marathon. Sweat formed at the back of my neck when I imagined his perfect body on top of mine, making good on his word. I would resist at first, pretending that every thrust he gave wasn't the best sex I'd ever had, but when he made me come, it would be impossible to lie. He would push me until I admitted the truth...that I wanted him inside me again and again. I'd never felt that way with another man, that I couldn't get enough of him and wanted him in my bed every night. I suspected Hades would be the first, and that told me I should stay away from him. "That's presumptuous."

"Am I wrong?" He turned his body closer to mine, bringing us in such proximity that we must look like lovers to everyone in the room, like two people who'd been fucking for weeks.

Past his shoulder I could see the woman still sitting there, watching Hades press his advance on a different woman. She'd been his focus of attention until the moment he lay eyes on me, and she probably couldn't figure out what went wrong. Seeing her pain and confusion made me feel guilty for being the other woman, for essentially stealing him away. "Yes."

His eyes softened slightly, like that was an answer he never imagined I would give.

"You should get back to your girl, Hades. She's waiting for you." I opened my clutch and fished out cash to leave on the table.

He didn't look over his shoulder. "I don't have a girl."

"The woman you were with just minutes ago."

"She's not my girl. Just met her."

"Well, ignoring her and pursuing someone else is rude." I slid out of the booth and didn't look back as I walked away. I didn't care if he was a playboy. I didn't care if he would fuck someone else the night after he fucked me. It was none of my business. But I wasn't interested in a man that could be so mercilessly rude. I walked outside and started the journey home.

He emerged behind me minutes later, as if he debated going after me before he rose from his seat. His loud footsteps were audible on the cement behind me, his dress shoes giving a distinct tap that I recognized.

He moved in front of me and cut off my path. On his feet and in front of me, he was a big man, bigger than he was when he was sitting beside me in the booth. He was over a foot taller than me, and with a muscle mass that made mine pathetic. He could squish me if he wanted to, choke me with a single hand and leave me for dead on the sidewalk. His eyes shifted back and forth quickly as he looked into my gaze, like he was livid with the way I walked away from him.

I bet no one ever walked away from him.

"I'm not done with you."

"Well, I'm done with you." I stepped around him.

He grabbed me by the arm and forced me back.

I twisted out of his grasp and stepped back. "Touch me again and see what happens."

My tough threat only made him smile. It was a slight grin, where only one corner of his mouth lifted. "I'd love that, actually. But I'm a gentleman...for the most part." He slid his hands into his pockets, as if he wanted to prove his sincerity. "Come over."

I'd never met a man so arrogant in my life. "Why would I want to come home with you?"

"So we don't have to finish this conversation on the sidewalk."

"There's no conversation to finish."

His smile faded away and his eyes turned hostile once more. "I met that girl ten minutes before I noticed you sitting there. I don't owe her a damn thing. If I didn't see you across the bar, I probably would have taken her home and fucked her. But I saw you... and I'm a lot more interested in you. If she got her feelings hurt, that's too bad. Don't hate the player, hate the game."

"Why would you be more interested in me?" I crossed my arms over my chest, my clutch still in my fingertips. "She was rubbing your dick and whispering dirty shit in your ear. She was a slam dunk."

"I don't need a slam dunk. My life is a fucking slam dunk."

"Wow...conceited much?"

"I'm blunt." He stepped closer to me, his hands remaining in his pockets like restraints. "I'm more interested in you because you're the most beautiful woman I've ever seen. When I saw you four years ago, I thought the same thing. I knew you would grow into your features, become a confident and sexy woman that owns the streets she struts down. Now here you are...and I want you."

All I had to do was say yes. I could be naked in his bed in minutes. My legs could be wrapped around his waist and I could lick the sweat off his chest. I wanted him four years ago and I still wanted him now. "It's not going to happen, Hades."

His head tilted slightly, like my words were nonsense.

"We're associates. I'm not entirely sure what you do for Gustavo, but one day, you and I will be working together. I don't shit where I eat."

He continued to stare at me, like he didn't hear a word I said. "You'll change your mind."

"I highly doubt it." Even if he didn't work with my family, he seemed like bad news. He seemed like a man that would capture my soul and shatter it. He was the kind of man that would ruin all other men. He would be fun for just a night, but anything more would just be detrimental to my health.

He stepped closer to me, bringing our faces so close to one another that his breath fell across my skin. He kept his eyes focused on mine, his scent surrounding me like a blanket. When I didn't inch back, he moved further in and placed his forehead against mine.

I should leave.

But I stayed.

He turned his head slightly, his eyes still on mine, and then he leaned in and kissed me. It was a soft contact between our lips, two pillows touching on a bed. When he moved his mouth I could feel the coarse touch of his facial hair, the way it tickled me as it scraped against my skin. The kiss was innocent, slow and tender like our mouths were getting to know each other. He felt my lips with purpose, sucked on my bottom lips softly before he released. Then he felt me again, filling me with his sexy warm breath. His hands remained in his pockets just to prove a point.

All I had to do was pull away but I couldn't. A simple kiss from him was intoxicating, addicting. It was so slow and gentle, nothing like our last embrace. He slowed down like we had all the time in the world to treasure it.

My hand slid up his forearm and felt the bicep in his thick arm. I kept going until I felt his chest, felt my fingers dig into his shirt the way that other woman did. Now I didn't care if he was rude when he ditched her for me. All I cared about was having him for myself. His kiss was better than sex, and if he was this good at kissing...imaging how good he was at fucking.

He pulled back, taking his delicious lips away from mine. Gloat was in his eyes as he looked at me, like he proved the point he wanted to make—a million times over. He held my look for a few more seconds, let the desire dissolve into my blood. "You'll change your mind."

Order now to keep reading